Text Classics

DON CHARLWOOD was born in Melbourne in 1915 and raised in Frankston, the background for his much-loved novel *All the Green Year* (1965), which was later made into an ABC TV series. During the Depression he walked through Victoria's Otway forest to the Western District, where he worked as a farmhand and began writing.

Charlwood joined the RAAF and served with Bomber Command in Britain during World War II, an experience that informed his first book, *No Moon Tonight*, published in 1956 and in print ever since. He then worked for thirty years in Air Traffic Control and the Department of Civil Aviation. When he retired in the mid-1970s an award for the air traffic control trainee of the year was named in his honour.

In 1978 Charlwood delivered the memorial oration for the centenary of the wreck of the *Loch Ard* and published *Settlers Under Sail*, commissioned by the Victorian government. *Marching as to War* (1990) and *Journeys into Night* (1991), two volumes of autobiography, each won the Fellowship of Australian Writers (Vic.) Christina Stead Award. Aged ninety Charlwood published *The Wreck of the Sailing Ship Netherby*.

In 1992 Don Charlwood was made a Member of the Order of Australia (AM) for services to Australian literature. He died on 18 June 2012.

MICHAEL McGIRR, the author of *The Lost Art of Sleep* and *Bypass: The Story of a Road*, is the head of faith and mission at St Kevin's College in Melbourne.

All the Green Year
Don Charlwood

Text Publishing Melbourne Australia

textclassics.com.au
textpublishing.com.au

The Text Publishing Company
Swann House
22 William Street
Melbourne Victoria 3000
Australia

First published by Angus & Robertson 1965
This edition published by The Text Publishing Company 2012

Cover design by WH Chong
Page design by Text
Typeset by Midland Typesetters

Printed in Australia by Griffin Press, an Accredited ISO AS/NZS 14001:2004
Environmental Management System printer

Primary print ISBN: 9781922079428
Ebook ISBN: 9781921961724
Author: Charlwood, D. E. (Donald Ernest), 1915-2012.
Title: All the green year / Don Charlwood.
Series: Text classics.
Subjects: Teenage boys—Victoria—Fiction.
Dewey Number: A823.3

CONTENTS

Years of Many Colours
by Michael McGirr

YOU won't travel far among Australian readers of a certain age before affectionate memories of *All the Green Year* begin to surface. More than that, the memories will be specific rather than vague. For two decades the novel was a regular feature of high school English, studied by people usually between the ages of thirteen and fifteen. Don Charlwood enjoyed one of the things that writers most covet: thousands of young readers, who often form deep and lasting relationships with books in a way not common in adult years. By that stage we have either read too much or read too little.

Nevertheless, forcing books into teenagers' hands is not always the best way to win their affections. A visitor to any op shop will find copies of *Othello* and *King Lear* treated with chastening contempt and consigned to the fifty-cent bin. Either they will be covered in graffiti (which suggests that even Shakespeare failed to interest the original owners) or they will have a few sections underlined with highlighters of different colours (which suggests that the owners were really interested in passing an exam). I once looked at a copy of *Great Expectations* whose cover had been altered to *Great Expectorations*. I won't mention what the owner had done with the name of Dickens and I feared I could find worse inside but, unsurprisingly, the contents had never been troubled. Bibles get the same treatment.

Before this welcome re-publication of *All the Green Year*, a beautiful evocation of Australian childhood first published in 1965, you might have been forced into op shops in the hope of finding it. But you will be amazed how many people, now well into middle age, have held on to their copies from long ago. Those deceptively small books, often with glued spines that tended to fall apart, will have moved with them from house to house as they got older, long after *The Web of Life* (the biology text of the same period) and *Good News for Modern Man* (the New Testament with the funky denim cover) had been donated to Vinnies or the Brotherhood.

But each time many of the baby boomers moved house, they would have looked at *All the Green Year* and felt a tug on their heartstrings. For many of them, it will have been the only book they read at school that dealt with their own experience in a way they could recognise.

It is set in 1929, which is more likely to have been the time in which their parents grew up, a world in which radio and gramophone cast the shadows that TV was to cast in their own time. The book deals largely with the experience of boys but has always been popular with female readers. It is set in Kananook—a fiction-alised version of Frankston, on the south-eastern fringe of Melbourne, at a time when the area was rural. By the sixties it was urban.

Despite this, *All the Green Year* is poised beautifully at that moment of adolescence when the small world of childhood suddenly becomes much bigger, with all the risk and sense of adventure that entails. It is a book with one foot in the air, hovering between innocence and its opposite, between the comfort of home and the dangerous lure of the horizon. For all this, the setting around Port Phillip Bay provides an evocative backdrop, as a place both familiar and threatening:

> Lone Pine had been named by Squid after a tree from which his father had sniped during the war...It had been planted by some forgotten settler on the highest ground of the district.
>
> Johnno and I began climbing without a word, putting our hands and feet in familiar places. At first the lower limbs hid the ground, but near the top the whole country opened from Point Nepean to Donna Buang...I could see the narrow gap of the Heads and the beginning

of the ocean and the pale, small lighthouse at Point Lonsdale. The sun was shining on the beaches, but no sound of waves reached us and no sound from the people who were distant specks in the water there.

Not long before this re-publication Don Charlwood died, aged ninety-six. Earlier in the year he was still an engaging and precise raconteur. He could claim a writing career spanning more than eighty years. This must be some kind of record, possibly rivalled in Australian literature only by Mary Gilmore or Rosemary Dobson. In April 2012 Charlwood published a substantial essay, 'They prohibited the future', for Anzac Day in his local paper, the *Warrandyte Diary*. It was also printed in all the Mornington Peninsula *News* papers, as 'Sole Survivor Remembers'. In the essay he returned to the theme of his first book, *No Moon Tonight*, published in 1956, which described the experience of the crews of Bomber Command in World War II, men who faced 'nearly an inevitable fate'.

Charlwood volunteered to join the air force in 1941, mainly because the son of the family with whom he was working on a property at Nareen in Victoria's Western District had also volunteered. Bomber Command led to some of the most significant relationships of Charlwood's life, not least with his wife, Nell East, whom he met and married in Canada in a case, he said with spry good humour, of love at first sight. But *No Moon Tonight* is alive with sadder memories. Among the grim statistics that remain with Charlwood is that twenty men enlisted alongside him; only five of them survived the war.

The silver lining to this horror was that, in being moved to honour the memories of his comrades, Charlwood was able to fulfil a personal ambition. Ever since he was at school, he dreamed of being a writer. Poems such as Tennyson's 'Ulysses' meant a great deal to him. But even more significant was Coleridge's 'Rime of the Ancient Mariner'. Charlwood loved the idea of being like the mariner, metaphorically grabbing the hand of an anonymous stranger and fascinating them with a tale, so much so that they couldn't move.

While he was working on the land in the 1930s he completed a short-story course by correspondence with the London School of Journalism and had a number of stories published, sometimes under the pseudonym E. K. Dwyer. For his twenty-first birthday he received a copy of Drinkwater's *Outline of Literature and Art*, which he used to choose the books that the state library would send to Nareen. These works fed his longing to tell stories of his own.

But, he explained, it was not until he was part of a lucky minority that survived the war that Charlwood found himself in the position of the Ancient Mariner, in possession of a story he felt compelled to share. Even after the phenomenal success of *All the Green Year*, a book which holds a special place in the lives of so many readers, Charlwood said that *No Moon Tonight* was his personal favourite. 'Because,' he said simply, 'it is a book of sorrow and companionship.'

All the Green Year followed *No Moon Tonight* after an interval of nine years and is a very different work. *All the Green Year* celebrates the invincibility of youth. The young characters have physical confidence and their story, despite its many challenges, is told with a lighter heart. There is a sense in which the book is a balm for the hurt of war. This is not to say that war is absent from it. Indeed, World War I casts a shadow in different parts of the novel: there is even a character called Birdwood Monash Peters ('Squid'), whose dad was supposedly killed at Gallipoli. *All the Green Year* also deals in good measure with the theme of male friendship, and with grief and loss. But in changing the original title from *Johnno's Year* (which his publisher did not like) to *All the Green Year*, the author surely understood the charm of his creation. The book has a wise innocence. It knows what life was like after the Great War, during the Depression, for boys in fear of bullying teachers and infatuated by pretty ones, at a time when adult life beckoned yet a livelihood was hard to come by. It also knows what it is like to be a boy with an open heart but a lot to learn.

All the Green Year may well have its origins in

Charlwood's first published work. By 1929 young Don had moved from East Hawthorn to Frankston, where his history teacher, Mr Moody, assigned him the task of writing a history of his new town. His mother, who had grown up in Frankston, drew up a list of senior residents of the district and Charlwood set off to interview them. The resulting oral history appeared in instalments in the *Frankston Standard*. Charlwood was just fourteen, and was already investing his imagination in the Frankston of that era.

More importantly, his writing career began from a discovery of the relationship between people and place. By 1965, when Don came to write *All the Green Year*, he and Nell had four children, including two teenage daughters. The world was full of The Beatles and the Vietnam War. One night Charlwood threatened to put his noisy girls in a book to serve them right. But, when he thought about it, he knew he couldn't. So he turned back to another time to write a wonderful story about boys. In so doing, he made a unique contribution to the exploration of boyhood in Australian writing, a rich vein that stretches at least from Norman Lindsay's *Redheap* (1930) and *Saturdee* (1933) to Craig Silvey's *Jasper Jones* (2009).

For all its quintessential Australianness, Don Charlwood's voice is very much his own. It is strong, resonant, compassionate, unsentimental and yet affectionate. Thank heavens we get to hear it again.

All the Green Year

For my mother, born in Frankston 17th May 1886.
Thank you for our years of growing up
in the town of your youth.

CHAPTER ONE

The year I remember best from those days is 1929.
This was the year I turned fourteen and went into the
eighth grade; the year too that Grandfather McDonald
became peculiar and we moved to live with him in his
house on the cliffs.

It has stayed in my memory for various reasons,
but chiefly for the fiasco at its end. I feel tempted to
claim that each incident played its part in leading
to our final disgrace, but this would hardly be true. The
matter of riding to school on Perry Brothers' camel,
for instance, had no link with later happenings at all,
nor did Squid's hypnotism, nor even, I suppose, the
preservation of Eileen Johnston's honour. These were
just isolated happenings linked with nothing. Looking
back at this distance of time it is difficult to recall which

of them came first, though for some reason it is easy enough to remember the people and more or less what they said.

During 1928 I had worn apple-catchers, but my main Christmas present had been a pair of long 'uns. My father said he hoped that now I was dressing as a man I would behave as a man. A forlorn hope this proved to be!

Both at home and at school at this time we felt ourselves badly misunderstood. Looking back I realize how serious everything seemed; only in retrospect does there appear a jot of humour in the whole year.

After five grades together this was my last year with Fred Johnston, a tall, melancholy boy of extraordinary physique, the son of a widower who ran Navy Bike Repairs in Beach Street. Though Johnno looked awkward when he tried to fit into a desk, or when he marched into school, head and shoulders above everyone else, as a swimmer and boxer hardly anyone in the town could touch him. He had learnt boxing from his father who at one time during the war had been R.A.N. welterweight champion. Old man Johnston was a shortish ex chief petty officer with a prominent blue-polished chin and eyes like agates.

About Johnno himself there was a contradiction I have never forgotten. He had practically no physical fear, yet he was always afraid of his father and of old Moloney. Moloney had been headmaster then for about ten years. His fear of both of them went back a long way; back, I suppose, to the third grade when Johnno had lost his mother. About a year after that Moloney, in a temper, had hit Johnno across the face with the strap. Johnno had gone home and told his father and old man Johnston had given him a note to bring to school. But the note only told Moloney to give him more for not taking his punishment like a man.

Moloney was a little thin-lipped man of about fifty, a bachelor still. The white, bald top of his skull showed through greying hair and he wore fairly thick-lensed spectacles. He had made a butt of Johnno for as long as I could remember—for instance, when we had begun to learn carpentry he had forced Johnno to use his tools as a right-hander when he was naturally left-handed, then had ridiculed his attempts to make anything.

In school Johnno was often afflicted by what he called "seizing up". If Moloney stood near him during a test, he became incapable of reasoning. Or during mental arithmetic when Moloney called, "Stand by your desks. Hands on your heads," Johnno was beaten before the question was written on the blackboard. When Moloney finally shouted "Write!" Johnno would sometimes remain with his hands fixed to his head and would move only when Moloney said, "I perceive you don't intend co-operating today, Johnston."

For both of us 1929 was critical, since at the end of the year we were to sit for our Merit. We had been assured

3

by Moloney that without it we would not be admitted to the third form of the new school just being built on the edge of the town. The name of this imposing building could be read in bold letters above its door, KANANOOK AND DISTRICT HIGH SCHOOL.

I should perhaps remark that in these days I was not even ordinarily adventurous or undisciplined; in fact Moloney's report described me as "inattentive and addicted to daydreaming". Johnno on the other hand he called "unconforming and a generally disruptive influence", this written so savagely that the nib had punched right through the paper. My report was true, but Johnno's was ridiculous.

My father naïvely believed Moloney's reports. Even when a boy called Birdwood Peters was named "most improved pupil for 1928" my father believed it and wished I would cultivate his friendship. At school no one doubted that Squid had won this prize because his mother, a widow, had been president of the Mothers' Club for five years; indeed there were people who said that Moloney had designs on her.

Unfortunately we were fated in 1929 to have the same Squid Peters as a neighbour; this in fact was one of a series of events that started the year badly.

Our move next to Squid's place came about in an odd way. It happened that in the previous year my grandmother had died, leaving my grandfather living alone in his old wooden house on the cliffs—the place in which

4

my mother had lived as a girl. It was just before Christmas 1928 that Grandfather became peculiar.

I should perhaps qualify this. To me Grandfather McDonald had seemed a little peculiar for as long as I could remember. He had for years called himself a Tolstoyan. I realize now that he must have been a Tolstoyan with variations of his own. For instance, although he was a vegetarian he would eat no apples because this was forbidden in the book of Genesis. A photograph of Tolstoy in the old house could almost have passed as Grandfather, with the same beard and stern, determined expression.

Anyway, when he became peculiar my mother had to go back and forth to "Thermopylae" to clean the place and cook him an occasional meal. He usually muttered and growled at her while she worked, or else sat out on the veranda to watch for passing ships—he had been an old Port Phillip pilot and before that a master in sail.

Under the house he had a collection of nautical odds and ends, and from this he had resurrected the wheel of the *Arabella*, a schooner wrecked years before somewhere off the Victorian coast. He fixed this to the veranda rail and standing there would steer the house towards the Heads, muttering and cursing and glaring at the horizon.

This of course didn't hurt anyone, and no one minded when he fitted the veranda with navigation lights and a binnacle. Complaints from Peters and other neighbours only began when he found a megaphone and used it to roar and blaspheme at ships out in the channel.

After a few months of this my mother said wearily, "It's not a bit of good—we can't watch him from here any longer. Either we'll have to go there, or he will have to come here to us."

From behind his newspaper my father muttered, "I'd sooner bring a grizzly bear to live here."

When my mother didn't answer him he sighed after a time and said, "Very well—we'll go, I suppose. I like the pater well enough, but I know nothing about ships or Tolstoy, or what's wrong with Darwinism—"

"It's a big house."

"It's ready to fall into the sea, I can tell you."

"But it was repaired not long ago."

My father lapsed into moody silence. After some time my mother said in a voice not intended for our ears, "It may be possible to put him in a home. Some people are doing this nowadays, you know. After all, it's hardly right for old people to live where there are young families."

My father threw down his paper. "For heaven's sake stop talking nonsense, girl! Did your father put you in a home when you were a squalling brat and he had to put up with you—did he now?"

My mother supposed not.

"No, he did what any decent human being should do—he looked after you. And now it's our turn to do the same for him. Anyhow, he'd tear a home apart."

My father was a rate collector with the council. He had gone to this job when he had come home from the war, and he didn't much like it. I recall that he was always studying for accountancy examinations to give him the opportunity of becoming shire secretary, but somehow his studying suffered frequent interruptions: my brother Ian was a bad sleeper when he was a baby; there was a prolonged family row with Aunt Ruby, then, in the fateful year of 1929, I interrupted him to an even greater degree than anyone. Anyway, when a new shire secretary was appointed my father was not selected and he went on all his life working as a rate collector and always felt he had failed. I realize now that he didn't fail at all in the things that mattered.

His own father had been a printer and bookseller in London. My father always referred to England as "Home"; in fact England was "Home" to most of our friends. It seemed a place tremendously far off to me, a place I always associated with the house in East Melbourne where my father had been born and where his mother still lived.

Grandfather McDonald on the other hand was a Scot, though he had come to Australia as a child. "Thermopylae" was over sixty years old and had probably only once been painted. It was high off the ground at the front and low against a hillside at the back. All around it was a wooden veranda, many of the boards by now loose. Inside was a large central living-room with the other rooms opening off it. In this room there were pictures of sailing ships and their bearded captains on every wall; also a sampler worked by Grandmother McDonald when she was a girl of twelve: WORK FOR THE NIGHT IS COMING. AGNES MCINTYRE 1860. All the inside walls were lined with tongued and grooved pine, and the whole place smelt old and musty. It creaked distinctly in high winds and was draughty even in a breeze. According to my father Grandfather McDonald liked to feel he was on the open deck, so to hell with comfort. Outside he had a flagpole from which he flew a flag on the King's Birthday, Anzac Day and various other commemorative occasions. It had once been the mast, I believe, of the same *Arabella*.

This was the house then that we were to live in during 1929.

CHAPTER TWO

I don't recall a great deal about the preparations to move to "Thermopylae" except that we let our house partly furnished to a family named Harris—Molly Harris was a girl at school. The arrival, though, I remember well.

Although Squid Peters lived next door this was not next door in the suburban sense, since the blocks along the cliffs were large and Squid's place was separated from Grandfather McDonald's by a barrier of tea-tree and a few large banksias, so that we could hardly see Peters' house at all. In a fork of a large banksia, at a height of about fifteen feet, Squid had made himself a platform where he sometimes sat Buddah-like, surveying the world. Unlike Buddah he was far from fat, in fact at thirteen there was nothing much of him but freckles and tow hair and a wary, but ingratiating expression. His father had been killed at the war. This was of course sad, nevertheless Squid didn't fail to capitalize on it. On Anzac Day he always laid a wreath the size of a lifebelt and wore more medals than George V. His most graphic story was of his father's rearguard action with the Turks while the rest of his battalion were being evacuated from Gallipoli. It was ten years before it struck me that Mr Peters must have left home at least eighteen months before Squid was born.

Squid's full name was Birdwood Monash Peters. The family had come from South Australia—"a State with some-think rather genteel about it," Mrs Peters said. She was a pianist with a genius for mood music, which she played by ear at the pictures. When Tom Mix or Buck Jones galloped across the prairies, she galloped up and down the keyboard without taking her eyes off the screen.

I was supposed, of course, to help with the move to "Thermopylae", though there was not a great deal to do, since the house was already furnished. We loaded the few things we needed on to one of Hopkins's lorries while the family walked in advance from home to Grandfather's. My father and mother walked in front, my father carefully raising his hat to everyone we met, then I came with Gyp on a lead, then came Ian, walking in the gutter, or breathing on shop windows so that he could write his "minitials". Kananook was by no means a large town in those days and pretty well everyone knew us.

When we arrived at "Thermopylae" I saw Squid sitting on his platform trying to screen himself behind leaves while he studied our possessions. I pretended not to have noticed him there and went on carrying things in without looking up. Now and again, if anything special came in, like the ice chest, he would glance down and whisper loudly to his mother, who was out of sight below, "A big ice chest," or "A crystal wireless." These were about the total of our luxuries.

I wandered over to him when we had finished, mainly to let him know we had seen him there. Before I could speak he said seriously, "Just as well you've come, I reckon."

I looked up irritably and asked why.

"Somethink wrong with your grandfather all right." He tapped his head sadly.

"He's just old," I said.

"Must be a bit barmy too, don't you reckon? No feller who wasn't barmy would shout at ships the way he does."

"He was a pilot down at the Heads—"

"I know; I know every ship he was ever on, I reckon. He yells it all out." All this he said dolefully, as if the case of Grandfather genuinely perturbed him.

We had not been talking long when Grandfather came onto the veranda. I moved downhill so that Squid would look away from the house, but it was no good. In a moment there was a fearful shout, "Ahoy, ye bluidy fool! Y' nearly on the bank."

There he stood, beard blowing in the breeze, eyes blazing, glasses swinging round his neck as he strode restlessly up and down.

"There, what did I tell you?" said Squid in an awed voice.

I could think of nothing to say. Grandfather went to the wheel, turning it a little this way and that. Because of the slope he was almost at Squid's level and about twenty yards behind us.

"Wear off, y' maniac."

I said defensively, "He's deaf and doesn't know he's shouting so loudly. Anyhow, the ships worry him—"

"There's not a ship in sight," said Squid mournfully. "Not a rowing boat—nothink."

I felt a wave of humiliation sweep over me. Then Grandfather suddenly spied Squid on his platform.

"You aloft there! On deck, or by God I'll flog the life out o' ye!"

An expression of shock passed over Squid's face, but with presence of mind he cried, "Ay, ay, sir!" while he backed hurriedly off his platform and let himself down by a rope into the tea-tree.

Grandfather came to the rail, ready to direct another blast at him, but just then my mother came and he allowed himself to be led inside.

12

CHAPTER THREE

When the door closed behind my grandfather I turned round and saw Squid's strained face looking out of the bushes.

"It's no good the way he carries on. It's got my mum scared stiff."

"You too," I said.

Every freckle on his face was standing out clearly. These freckles were usually part of his stock in trade. According to his mother they were the cause of his sensitiveness and my own mother had warned me not to mention them to him. All of which was nonsense, for he charged a penny for an inspection of the freckles on his back and twopence to inspect his stomach.

"You're scared yourself," I repeated.

He didn't answer. I could see him trying to think of something to restore his dignity. He was a past master at turning defeat into victory by thinking up something unusual. Sure enough it came.

Presently he said, "I been learning hypnotism." He looked at me from under lowered lids.

It was the sort of claim one could expect from Squid. "Baloney," I said.

He looked at me in a hurt way. "It's true. I got it out of a book loaned me by a Indian bloke like Gandhi."

"Try it on me, then," I said, staring at him.

He shook his head. "Too risky. You got blue eyes and the book says it could bring on brain fever for anyone with blue eyes."

"Try it on Gyp, then."

Before he could answer I whistled Gyp. He came from under the veranda and looked at us interestedly. He was a cross between a Labrador and a Kelpie—or we supposed he was—a large black dog who spent most of his days chasing seagulls or retrieving sticks, or on Guy Fawkes Night attacking crackers.

"Here, Gyp." He slobbered over me and sat down attentively. "Squid's going to hypnotize you."

He grinned and hung out his tongue.

Squid changed his mind. "No," he said gravely, "no, it could make him go mad. If he bit someone, then they'd go mad. It goes on and on."

Gyp looked disappointed. He lay in the sun and closed his eyes.

"There's one thing I can do—there's our chooks. If y' very good at it, y' can hypnotize chooks."

"All right," I said. "When do you start?"

He peered through the tangle of branches into his back yard. "Mum's down the street, I think." He threw a pebble on the iron roof and when this brought no protest he invited me through the gap in the fence.

Peters' yard was a jungle of tea-tree, a quiet place and always gloomy. The fowl-yard was at the edge of the cliff and in it a dozen Plymouth Rocks scratched half-heartedly.

"Better get going," I said tauntingly.

Squid looked hurt at my disbelief. I squatted outside the yard while he went in. The hens were so quiet that they hardly bothered getting out of his way. He scooped one up. It squawked feebly, but stopped as soon as he held it before his eyes and began murmuring some sort of gibberish.

This went on for some time, his voice rising and falling. I was beginning to regard the performance scornfully when he lowered the hen and swung it back and forth above the ground, using his arms like a pendulum; back and forth it went while his muttering rose in key till it sounded like a wail from a long way off. All at once he turned the hen on its back and lay it on the ground. It stayed there, its feet pointing at the sky, the stiffest hen I'd ever seen.

"Hell!" I breathed.

Squid ignored me and scooped up another. He stared into its eyes muttering the gibberish again, then began the swinging motion and in a minute a second hen lay beside the first. By the time he had put three in a row, all their feet stupidly in the air, he whispered, "I better stop. It fair takes the power outer me."

He waved his hands over the recumbent hens, fingers extended, then came out to me, his face haggard. The first hen presently recovered, got to its feet, wobbled a bit and began pecking the ground again.

"How do you do it?" I asked quietly.

He shook his head. "Some people has it, some hasn't." He looked at me closely. "With blue eyes you'd never have no hope—that's what the Indian feller in the book says."

The second hen struggled up and looked about glassily.

"When do I read the book?"

"I had t' give it back."

I looked into his freckled face, trying to tell whether he was making all this up, but he looked serious, a bit afraid even of his own power; besides, the last hen still lay on its back as evidence. He clapped his hands and after a second it lurched to its feet.

"Well," he said recovering himself, "I better chop the wood."

16

"Hang on—" I began.

But he left me with the air of a man to whom miracles were nothing. I never saw him repeat this particular miracle and I never really learnt the secret of it. It at least made the day of our move to "Thermopylae" a memorable one.

CHAPTER FOUR

There were five of us at "Thermopylae". My mother was the busiest and calmest one of us all, yet everything revolved around her. I see now that she had the knack of getting her own way almost effortlessly. Yet she was a shy woman and inclined to depression. Perhaps because she had lived all her life in Kananook and was known to everyone, she felt concerned always for the family's reputation: even to receive an account rendered from one of the local shopkeepers was to her like being accused of theft.

In those days I saw her in only one hat and with one handbag—this was at the beginning of the depression, of course, when most people we knew had to manage on little.

My father's clothing difficulties were no easier. Although his collars were always starched and shining, the patching of some of his shirts would not have allowed him to take off his coat, let alone his waistcoat, even had he thought this proper.

My father was no doubt a frustrated man, irked always by the lowly job he had. I heard him debate occasionally with Grandfather, just to please the old man, but I could never be sure what his views were. He would sing sometimes in the Church of England choir and sometimes Ian would sing there, too. Ian was nine then and had a soprano voice of such purity that anyone not knowing him would have thought him a paragon of holiness. When he sang something like "Oh, For the Wings of a Dove" he even convinced me; but then I would hear him singing it around the house while he tied Gyp and the cat together, or tried between breaths, to throw my marbles from the veranda into the sea.

My grandfather, the main character at "Thermopylae", I have already tried to describe. In his day he had been a great debater and liked to argue ferociously about such things as Darwinism, or the truths revealed in the Book of Revelations, or the curse of usury. By the time we came to "Thermopylae" his debating days were over and he spent hours at a time ruminating and rumbling to himself or sometimes flaring out with some startling question like, "And who was the Abomination of Desolation but Darwin?"

Though he stared challengingly at us he really expected no answers.

There was a slight burr to his speech. He had left Scotland as a boy and had never been back, but he spoke as bitterly about Culloden Moor and "the Royal Butcher" as if he had been at the battle himself.

I remember him best at the table, growling a Gaelic grace to himself, his mouth and whole beard moving. His jaw was larger on one side than the other, as he had been kicked in the face by a horse years before. His jaw had been set by Grandmother, since he didn't believe in calling doctors. My father always claimed that the horse had broken its leg—which could well enough have been true.

An old debating companion sometimes came to see him. This was Mr Theo Matthias, a man who was said to be a Bolshevik. He was given this label I think by my Aunt Ruby—of whom more later—after his flare-up one day in church. It had been Mr Matthias's habit for years to go to the vestry after Sunday morning service to argue about the sermon with the vicar. As he got older his arguments became more and more testy. At last one morning during the prayer for the King he stood up as Mr Timms reached, ". . . thy chosen servant George our King—" and declared, "Chosen poppy-cock!" and walked out, his short beard thrust forward like a tusk. From then on he was an established Bolshevik—an accusation that drove Grandfather to fury.

In the earlier twenties these two old men had gone fishing together each Saturday and it was said that when they were a mile out in the channel you could hear their voices from "Thermoplyae's" veranda.

Grandfather's boat was now only a relic of those days. It slept in its decrepit shed at the foot of the cliffs. Occasionally I was allowed to take it out, but I knew hardly anything of seamanship, even though I had lived by the Bay all my life.

The cliffs below "Thermopylae" were not true cliffs; at least, they were neither sheer nor rocky. Their sloping face was covered with thick vegetation, all bent inland. Down through the twisted trees a few tunnel-like tracks zigzagged to the sand.

Near the top of the cliffs the house perched like an aged sea-bird. It had little in the way of conveniences, though I daresay it was no worse than most houses in the town. We had only a chip bath-heater and a chip copper and no septic sewerage. Ian always believed Hell to be under the little house by the fig-tree, and it was difficult to induce him to remain there long.

Bath night was Saturdays, but I was supposed to follow my father's example of a daily cold shower, even when the shower had to be thawed with a candle. The only way to escape in winter was to put no more than a leg under and make gasping noises.

In my mother and father's room and Grandfather's room too, there were dignified-looking jugs standing in washbasins, and of course there were the other pieces of chinaware as well.

For drinking-water "Thermopylae" had tanks, not because Kananook was without a town supply, but because Grandfather was sure the town water had been tampered with by Jennings the shire engineer.

It was decided I would sleep under Grandfather's window on the north veranda, which was the side of the house least exposed to the weather. Even though thick tea-tree protected it, there were nights when the canvas blinds flapped wildly and the roar of waves sounded so close that I would find myself dreaming we were out at sea. These were the nights Grandfather was likely to get up and take the helm. Once or twice on windy moonlit nights I saw him, beard and hair blowing, pyjamas clinging about him, the ghost of a captain on a ghostly ship. The only way to handle him then was for my father to run outside crying, "Ready to take over, sir." Then Grandfather would relinquish the wheel and allow my mother to lead him back to bed.

But these nights weren't frequent. Usually the Bay was calm and from my bed I could hear the lapping of waves on the beach at the base of the cliffs. Sometimes on these still nights I could hear through the thin wall Grandfather debating Darwinism with himself, taking first one side and then the other. Darwin always lost.

At the dinner table he would sometimes brood and mutter to himself and then, in the middle of someone's conversation roar out, "He tol' men they were monkeys, an' by God they've been behaving like monkeys ever since."

My father asked him once if it really mattered whether God had created the world through Adam and Eve, or through a system of evolution. Grandfather glared at him and stormed, "Ye dispute then the Holy Writ?"

I suppose my father was patient to put up with life at "Thermopylae". Not many men, after all, could have been required in the one night to debate Darwinism and to take over a ship with no training.

Out on the veranda the sun would wake me early. The sea then was usually so calm that a cape beyond "Thermopylae" would lie reflected on its surface. It was easy then to imagine the first explorers coming there and Buckley the Wild White Man walking alone around the beach. The only sound at that hour was the whirring of Squid's pigeons. He kept these more for profit than pleasure; double profit often, as some always came back to him after he had sold them.

And from the kitchen I would hear Grandfather's mantel clock rapidly striking the hour. It was an old Ansonia with cherubs on its glass and a hurrying silver pendulum. Even now I associate its striking with sounds of the sea. All that year it marked our hours, the frustrated hours of my father, the worried hours of my mother, the final hours of Grandfather McDonald.

CHAPTER FIVE

On the last day of the holidays my mother told me it would be nice if I were to walk to school next morning with Birdie.

"He's such a nervous boy. He worries so terribly over his poor freckled face."

I knew it was no good ridiculing him; at our place Squid was a kind of freckled saint. I suppose I looked unhappy at the idea of walking with him, because my father said sharply, "You don't seem to appreciate decent companions."

I wasn't sure what to answer to this, so I said nothing.

"Let me tell you this." My father put his book of accountancy down. "This year is your last chance. If you don't do well, you'll have no hope at all of getting a job; you'll be out swinging a pick with your friend Johnston. There will be hundreds begging for jobs."

Poor old Johnno, I thought. He tried hard enough, but everyone was against him. I pictured him swinging his pick while Squid drove by in a car. Squid was born lucky. He planned to become an estate agent, or a stockbroker. There was no doubt he would do well in whatever he took up—someone else would do the work while he got the money. What a life he had! Pictures free while his mother played the piano; favouritism from Moloney; a new bike for Christmas.

I heard my father's voice droning on. It occurred to me that the worst of parents was the misery they caused by worrying about the future. Why were they like this? Why did they have families if it was all worry? I would never get married, that was certain. Imagine being tied to a woman for ever, and for ever worrying about money.

My father's nose was suddenly an inch from mine, his eyes blazing. He roared, "Why don't you answer my question? Here I've been trying to help you and what do you do? You stare into space and think about heaven knows what."

"Yes," I said, several times. "Yes, yes."

"What was I saying?"

"About money—"

He gave an exasperated snort, leapt to his feet and stamped into the kitchen. I heard him there shouting to my mother, "That boy will drive me to lunacy. D' you

26

hear? I'm damn' sure no one in our family was ever like this. How is he going to get any further at school? What sort of dumb, good-for-nothing generation are we bringing up?"

He slammed the door and strode outside. My mother came in to me, wiping her hands slowly on her apron, her face concerned.

"You heard that?"

It seemed that everyone in the town must have heard it.

"What are you going to do about it?"

"I don't know," I burst out. "I'm sick of life. No one except Johnno understands what it's like. I never have any time to do what I want to do—"

"What is it you want to do?"

I wasn't sure of this. As I groped for an answer my mother said, "Swim and go out with Fred Johnston?"

I replied hotly, "That would be better than working for old Moloney, anyhow."

"Listen," she said quietly, "your father sees the mistakes he has made and he wants to save you some of them—"

I said bitterly, "It'd be better fun making my own mistakes."

My mother sighed and went back into the kitchen and I went to bed. I fell asleep making elaborate plans to run away.

I escaped Squid in the morning as he had decided to ride his new bike. School was about a mile from "Thermopylae". You could either go past the park and along beside the Mechanics' Hall, or straight through the bush to the bottom of the school ground. All that year I seldom had more than ten minutes to cover the distance, so I usually had to go the short way.

At the end I would come out of the bush and see the brownish brick building on its hill, looking like something designed by an architect of prisons. There were trees around it, but the ground between them was worn by the trampling of feet and their trunks were rubbed bare.

In the unlikely event of being early I would see ahead of me the trickle of other pupils going to school, a trickle like a creek almost dried up and reluctant to flow.

When I was late the grounds would be accusingly empty and an industrious hum would rise from the classrooms. If it was a Monday I might hear the Declaration being chanted, "I love God and my country; I honour the flag, I serve the king and cheerfully obey my parents, teachers and the law." "Cheerfully obey"! Cheerfully obey old Moloney!

There he was on that hot February morning squinting through his glasses, nose screwed up, nicotine-stained teeth clenched, scalp white, moustache cut so short that you weren't sure whether it was a moustache or whether he had forgotten to shave for a few days; butterfly collar making marks on his neck; wooden-handled strap in pocket.

A blast on his whistle and Squid began to beat the drum importantly while we marched in.

"Ah, Reeve, you have come back?"

"Yes sir."

"You intend working this year, I trust?"

"Yes sir."

"I think we shall sit you at the front where I can ensure you are awake and not merely pretending."

"Yes sir."

"Well stop 'yes-sirring' and sit down."

I sat at the ink-stained desk which had been carved and scratched and rubbed for fifty years or more. All the examination suffering of generations was stored in its dirty, brownish wood. On the blackboard in big letters was MERRY CHRISTMAS, left from six weeks earlier as if to mock us. Dead flowers were still in a vase, and over the blackboard our one picture was covered with dust. This was a picture of Sappho's head, Sappho being, we understood, a goddess of Roman times.

While Stinger Wray, the ink monitor, moved from desk to desk, Moloney set about making up the roll. He had reached the Rs when Johnno appeared in the doorway, twenty minutes late. There had been a crisis at his place because a coat someone had passed on to him was short in the sleeves. His sister Eileen had let the sleeves down, but the effect was worse. The fold lines showed clearly and the uncovered material contrasted with the rest of the coat.

Johnno stood at the door with his large hands protruding from the sleeves. His huge chest was heaving and the usual strand of ginger hair kept falling over his right eye. At fifteen he looked too old for the eighth grade, in fact too old for school at all. He had deep-set, distant eyes, a look of patience in them, but not of much hope. Moloney left him standing there while he began checking everyone's supply of new books. The smell of these books and of sharpened pencils hung in the air—the new uneasy, beginning-of-year smell.

After several minutes Johnno said, "Please sir—"

Moloney, pretending he had not seen him till then, faced round quickly. "What do you mean—'please sir'?"

"Please sir, I'm late," said Johnno.

"Well, well," replied Moloney. "It struck me that the rest of us might have been early." Some of the girls tittered. "You have a note?"

"No sir."

"Why not?"

"There wasn't time, sir."

"Wasn't time?"

"My sister had to do something for me."

"A big man to make his sister an excuse. A big man," he repeated, half turning to the class.

Johnno flushed and moved his feet uneasily. No one had been told more often than he had been that he was no good, that he could never do anything. There was no boy more unsure of himself in school.

Moloney rubbed his chin. "I think, Johnston, that since you need a woman's tender care, we shall sit you for today next to Janet Baker—if Janet has no objection."

Janet was so short-sighted that she had difficulty in seeing if anyone was next to her at all, but she moved on principle to the far side of the desk while Johnno struggled to get his knees under it and sit down.

Moloney stared at us for several moments with a mirthless smile. "This year you will be sitting for the Merit Certificate and I intend having no failures. You hear that, Reeve?"

"Yes sir."

"And Johnston?"

"Yes sir."

"I can't imagine how you're going to reach this standard, Johnston," he added, "but reach it you shall. Now I propose that we have a test once a week, every Monday morning as soon as you arrive; mental arithmetic, dictation, grammar—"

The list went on alarmingly.

"You will correct each other's work; but twice a month I shall take up the papers and check your marking. I shall certainly not tell you when this is to be—'Ye will know neither the day nor the hour'."

A tremor passed over the class. It was hard to believe you could go so quickly from freedom to slavery.

I glanced to one side and saw the same faces as last year—and I can see them yet: Fat Benson who each month grew heavier—probably because he lived behind Fry's sweets shop by the Palais; Stinger Wray who was always self-important, possibly to make up for his mother's persistent yelling at him; Windy Gale, whose mother and father hadn't spoken to each other for years—he had to carry notes from one to the other and had to get his father out of pubs. It was Stinger's father who had a system by which he was going to win a fortune at the races. Near the back was Pommy Ellison—not a pommy really; it was just that his parents spoke "correctly", as my father put it, and Pommy had brought this unfortunate habit to school. And, of course, there was Squid, basking in Moloney's favour.

The girls were a blur of dresses and giggles and self-possession. As I glanced at them it struck me that they looked better than the previous year. Perhaps it was the way hair was caught behind ears and arms emerged from short sleeves and new plumpnesses were exhibited.

The silence roused me. I heard Moloney's level voice saying, "I repeat, Reeve: do you fancy yourself as a Don Juan?"

I faced him quickly.

"What was I discussing?" he demanded.

"I'm—not sure, sir."

"Not sure. Not sure! Reeve, for as long as I've known you you've never been sure of anything—and you never remain attentive long enough to *make* sure of anything."

He took out the wooden-handled strap. "Come out here."

A year of this, I thought; a year of cheerfully obeying!

CHAPTER SIX

At lunch-time in those days Johnno and I would climb
the post-and-rail fence at the bottom of the school ground
and wander across a grey, sandy road into the bush. There
was a grassy clearing a hundred yards in, and this was
where we ate lunch and in winter had boxing practice.

After the glare and heat that first day the clearing was
cool. We lay at full length on the grass and unwrapped
the newspaper from around our sandwiches.

"What've you got?" I asked.

"Two dripping and one sugar," he said.

Eileen was not an imaginative maker of sandwiches.

"I'll swap you a tomato for a dripping."

We ate lying on our sides enclosed by motionless
trees, Moloney and the school shut away, the voices
from the school ground an indistinct babel.

We knew every track of this country. For years we had had lunch-time chases through the miles of bush, Johnno and I pursued by the rest of the grade, I the dispatch-bearer, he the escort. Sometimes we would lie hiding in the undergrowth while the searchers moved a few feet away. I would feel as tense then as if our lives had really been at stake. But this year the idea of chases seemed vaguely childish.

When we had finished lunch Johnno said, "What about boxing practice? I've changed my style a bit—more like Billy Grimes." He stood up and flexed his arms.

"Too hot," I said. "Let's walk across to Lone Pine."

"Okay, then."

We started slowly, saying little.

Lone Pine had been named by Squid after a tree from which his father had sniped during the war. The track went steeply downhill, the bush about it growing thicker as it neared a small creek. We drank at a dark pool which Squid had told me years before was bottomless. From there the track climbed steeply to the hilltop where the pine stood dark against the sky. It had been planted by some forgotten settler on the highest ground of the district.

Johnno and I began climbing without a word, putting our hands and feet in familiar places. At first the lower limbs hid the ground, but near the top the whole country opened, from Point Nepean to Donna Buang. We sat on a board seat we had nailed there, feeling the trunk swaying us gently. I could see the narrow gap of the Heads and the beginning of the ocean and the pale, small lighthouse at Point Lonsdale. The sun was shining on the beaches, but no sound of waves reached us and no sound from the people who were distant specks in the water there.

"The public-school kids are still on holidays," said Johnno aggrievedly.

There seemed no justice in life at all. While others swam at our beach, we suffered Moloney.

Inland, all the secrets of streets and yards were open to us: lines of washing; a cable tram which was Mrs Kelly's sleep-out; old Charlie Rolls' tent that his wife made him sleep in; wood-heaps; horses outside Jonas's livery stable. A cab moved slowly down Bay Street and someone chased after it and leapt on the back step. If Dan Weekly was the driver, he would lash round with his whip and yell abuse and look angrily through the little window. In those cabs if no one called "Whip behind!" and the driver didn't see you, you could climb in and lie on the mat on the floor and feel the sway of the cab and hear the sound of hoofs and the running of the wheels on the road.

"If I fail in the Merit I'll run away," said Johnno darkly.

"You said you'd do that last year."

"Last year I had one more chance; this year I've got no more." He was staring unhappily towards the sea. After a bit he said, "In arithmetic, Charlie, my answers even look crazy, but I reckon I can write decent compositions." He looked at me anxiously round the trunk. "Can't I?"

"I reckon you can," I said—and this was true; in fact compositions were all either of us liked. Even when we thought we had done these well, Moloney would take half our marks for bad grammar, or split infinitives, or sentences ending with prepositions.

The faint sound of the first bell drifted up to us, so far off that it seemed nothing to take notice of. All the distant sounds from the school ground rose a little in key, as if everyone had called, "We've got to go in!" We were too far off to hear words. We could only hear occasional separate shouts, or girls squealing, or Squid practising the drum. The clusters at the cricket pitch and playing stick fly looked like a prison camp of microbes from which we had escaped.

As Johnno started down I cast a last glance on the houses and their rising smoke and on the few streets, and the Palais, the longest building in the town. This was where Mrs Peters played on Wednesdays and Saturdays. There was some sort of mystery about the distant town; some sort of apartness, as if now that the holidays were over it was closed to us. Once on the ground we began to run.

"Where would you go anyhow?"

"When?"

"If you ran away?"

"England—or maybe row across the bay to the Otways."

"You mean the You Yangs."

"The Otways are out there somewhere, too, not far across the Bay—forests they say, where a man could hide."

We had started up the hill and talking was no longer easy. "I wouldn't mind going with you," I said. But I knew that if it came to the point I would probably back out, nor did I realize Johnno had heard and would remember.

CHAPTER SEVEN

It must have been around this time that Johnno came to "Thermopylae" one Saturday morning. He seldom appeared at our place, probably because he sensed that my father thought him a ne'er-do-well.

He sat on the veranda steps. No, he wouldn't come in.

"Have you had breakfast, Fred?"

"Yes thanks, Mrs Reeve."

Behind us my grandfather was stepping slowly up and down the veranda, his glasses round his neck.

Johnno said, "Good morning, Captain McDonald."

Grandfather stopped and growled that it was no damn' good at all. After staring at us a while, he went on with his measured striding.

Johnno said quietly to me, "I've got bad news."

I led him round the side of the house away from Squid's place.

"I've got to go to a dance," he told me.

"Why?" It was hard to imagine anything more distasteful.

"My old man says I have to take Eileen. It's at the Mechanics' next Wednesday."

I said, "She's older than you are, why can't she take herself?"

"I don't know," he said, shaking his head. "It's to do with her—her honour."

"Her what?"

"Her honour."

This was something I had never heard mentioned outside poetry books.

"How?"

Johnno flung out his hand. "I don't know. I tried to ask my old man, but he got queer—said Eileen's sixteen and there are chaps round who might chase after her. I didn't get the hang of it at all."

I said, "Eileen could fight most chaps herself, anyhow."

"She's not bad," Johnno admitted. "Goes to pieces, though, when she loses her temper." He pondered glumly, then suddenly came to the point. "Would you come with me, do you reckon?"

I subsided slowly on to the ground. "Me? I don't know. I think dad wants me to . . . ." I couldn't think of anything he wanted me to do. I finished lamely, "I don't think I'd be allowed."

The idea filled me with horror. I saw a dance floor filled with couples expertly gyrating and Eileen and I . . . . It was impossible!

"Do you reckon you could ask?"

"My grandfather doesn't believe in it," I found myself saying. And this was true; at least he had once told me that the woman who had started the circular waltz had asked for John the Baptist's head on a plate.

"But how about your mother and father?"

"They wouldn't mind at all, Fred," said my mother's voice from the veranda. She was making my bed and I hadn't even seen her. "I think it's very nice indeed to find a boy taking his sister out."

As I groaned aloud I heard the breath come out of Johnno with relief. "Thank you," he said. "Thank you, Mrs Reeve."

I couldn't speak; I sat huddled on the lawn.

"And you see that you dance with Eileen, Charlie," said my mother as she went inside.

I looked at Johnno. "That was a lousy thing to do. You saw her and I didn't. How do you dance when you've never been taught anyway?"

Johnno didn't even answer this. "Hell, I'm glad you can come!" he exclaimed.

Unfortunately my father agreed with old man Johnston. I was to remember that Eileen had no mother to guide her. In any case it was right for a boy to escort his sister, and besides it might teach Fred a little pride in his manners.

"In my day a boy thought it a privilege—"

I didn't listen any more; I had heard it all before. When he had finished I said, "I thought you didn't want me to go out with Johnno."

"That's enough of that!" he snapped.

I dragged to Johnno's on the Wednesday evening in my best suit, my hair brushed and my boots cleaned. Johnno and his father were in the sitting-room, Johnno in his uncle's blue suit, his hair slicked back, his expression more than usually glum. Eileen hadn't appeared, but I could smell her perfume, an unnerving, overpowering smell. Old man Johnston rocked back and forth on his heels and toes studying Johnno narrowly. He was a good deal shorter than Johnno, but squarish-looking, his shining blue chin cloven at the centre. On his watch-chain was a medallion showing two boxers shaping up to each other.

"You understand now?"

"Yes sir," said Johnno, nodding anxiously.

"I've seen girls, young girls at that, leave the hall with men. It's no good."

"No," said Johnno vaguely.

"Remember now, she's your sister and a man should defend his sister's honour to the limit."

"Charlie," he said, turning his gimlet eyes on me, "I'm sure you will watch too that Eileen isn't prevailed upon—"

Eileen came out in the middle of this. I looked at her with my mouth open. It seemed ridiculous to think she was only two years older than I was, or to think I had boxed with her hardly a year before.

Mr Johnston gazed at her a long time, then he said in a quieter voice, "All right, now, home by twelve—and Eileen, be the woman your mother was."

All the way to the hall we walked reluctantly one on either side of her, our feet stirring up the dust. She said once to Johnno, "Do I look nice, Fred?"

"I don't know," he answered. "I haven't noticed."

"Charlie," she said, ignoring him, "how do you think I look?"

"Terrific," I admitted.

"Thank you. See, Fred?" Johnno didn't answer.

The night was calm and filled with moonlight, a good night for floundering or sitting on the end of the pier; a good night for almost anything but going to a dance. As we walked across the football ground, Eileen hummed "The Red Red Robin" and every now and then skipped as if she couldn't wait to get to the hall. In the moonlight I could see a smile on her face and see Johnno looking despondently at the ground.

"You boys really needn't worry about me," she said condescendingly.

"I'm not worrying about *you*," said Johnno morosely. "I'm only worrying what will happen if dad reckons I haven't looked after you."

She patted his cheek. "Dear brother!"

"Cut it out," he said. "You smell terrible."

"It's eau de Cologne," she said happily.

"Well, don't come too near us."

As we reached the other side of the football ground and walked across the park we could see the lights of the hall, ironically gay through the trees, then we heard the alarming *boompa, boomp, boomp* of music and a voice yowling,

> "*Yes, sir, that's my baby*
> *No, sir, don't mean maybe,*
> *Yes, sir, that's my baby now.*"

"Gawd!" muttered Johnno.

"Which of my partners will dance first with me?" asked Eileen.

I felt my stomach turn.

"I only said I'd bring you, "said Johnno immediately.

"I'm sure Charlie will dance, won't you Charlie?"

"I don't know how to," I said, scarcely above a whisper.

"Oh, you can foxtrot; anyone can foxtrot."

"No," I said, "No."

"I'll show you, Charlie."

My voice had deserted me. We were at the door by this and I could think of no way of escape. We handed in our tickets and went into the glare of lights. Half the town was there mooching now to something slow, the girls all eyeshadow and lipstick; the men expert-looking, among them some blazered public-school boys with long hair and pained accents.

> *"What'll I do-o*
> *When yo-u*
> *Are fa-r*
> *Awa-y-"*

"Wait now while I do my hair," ordered Eileen.

"It's done already," muttered Johnno.

She screwed up her nose at him and sailed towards the ladies' cloakroom.

Johnno looked after her bitterly. "I'd like to see her sit fair on her backside in front of everyone, that's what I'd like."

Finding my voice I said, "Johnno, I feel sick—"

"No," he said, grasping my arm. "No; you can't go, Charlie—"

"It's my stomach—"

"No, Charlie. Here, sit down." He pushed me into a seat at the edge of the crowd. "Afterwards we'll go to the supper-room—"

"I couldn't eat anything—not a thing."

The number ended and the crowd clapped. Eileen still hadn't appeared. Perhaps she was sick, too, I thought; perhaps it was something going around.

Everyone had left the floor when she came regally across to us, smiling right and left. She looked anything but sick.

"And how are my partners?"

"You're a damn' skite," said Johnno.

"Dear brother! Never mind, Charlie will look after me."

My voice had gone again.

"Take your partners for a foxtrot. This will be a tap dance."

The music started again, but I remained fixed to the seat. I had no idea what a tap dance was. The floor filled quickly with self-assured couples.

"Charlie, aren't we going to have this dance?"

I stood up in a trance and let Eileen lead me on to the floor. I raised my arm as if it belonged to someone else.

"Other arm," she whispered.

We shuffled away, her knees bumping mine and our feet tangling unbelievably. I had misunderstood the tap dance. Half-way down the floor a blazered collegian decorated with oars and Roman numerals tapped my shoulder.

"Your partner, if I may."

Eileen flung herself into his arms. "Thank you, Charlie."

I started back to Johnno, feeling suddenly better.

"Terrific," he breathed. "Terrific."

I wasn't sure what had been terrific, getting rid of Eileen or my performance, but I said, "It's easy enough once you get the idea."

This was all we had to do for Eileen. She became the centre of the public school circle and didn't so much as look our way. We drifted off to the supper-room and guarded her honour from a distance for the rest of the evening. She only came near us when the group came to supper. The oarsman took her arm and she moved unnecessarily close to him. Johnno looked at them and frowned, as if trying to decide whether or not this amounted to a threat to her honour. Eileen didn't even see us. She talked in a high-pitched, exaggerated voice about dances and parties she had attended.

"Wouldn't she make you sick? If it wasn't for the old man I'd clear off."

"She wouldn't care much," I said.

". . . a Riley," the oarsman was saying. "Had her up to eighty coming down . . . . Of course, any time— tonight if you like . . . . No, no, not at all . . . ."

I glanced at Johnno, but his face was submerged in cream cake. When I looked round again Eileen had gone. I touched Johnno's arm. "She's gone."

"Outside?"

"Must have."

We hurried to the door, but as we reached it a red Riley exploded beside the hall and went roaring up the road with a dramatic changing of gears.

Beside me Johnno groaned. "I'll be killed for this."

We went outside and began wandering anxiously up and down the road, hardly saying a word, Johnno with his shoulders bowed like an old man.

"When they come back I'll say, 'I'm here to defend—'"

"No," I said. "No, don't say that."

"Well what?"

"I don't know."

We sat in the black shadows of tea-tree on the far side of the road and cursed the whole arrangement. It was already half-past eleven, and by twelve we were supposed to be home. Johnno kept standing up and peering uselessly down the moonlit road.

At a quarter to twelve we heard the Riley coming. It rocketed up to the hall, skidding into the parking area in a cloud of dust. The engine stopped and we heard Eileen laugh, a high-pitched excited laugh. Then the lights were switched off and we could hear them murmuring. Johnno waited undecidedly, clenching and unclenching his fists. Then plainly we heard Eileen cry, "No, no, certainly not!"

Johnno bounded across the road and flung open the driver's door.

"I say—" exclaimed a surprised voice.

"I give you three to get out!" shouted Johnno. "One, two—"

The oarsman leapt out quickly and seized Johnno by the coat front. "Now, look here—"

That was the beginning. Johnno knocked his hand down and they were at it fiercely. Indoors the band was playing "Tiger Rag" as if trying to keep up with the blows. It was a fight worth watching; in fact I forgot Eileen until I heard her call out, "He's my brother! Stop it. Stop it! Oh Charlie, please stop them!"

She should have known Johnno was safe. He was rolling and dodging in his best Billy Grimes style, waiting patiently for his chance. Suddenly the oarsman doubled up and fell on his hands and knees, gulping horribly.

Eileen burst into tears. "It's all right," I said catching her arm. "Fred's beaten him."

She broke away from me and ran towards Johnno who was bending concernedly over his adversary. All at once she yelled at him, "I hate you! I hate you! I'll beat you myself."

I realized then that the band had stopped and that people were coming to the doors.

The oarsman staggered to his feet and lowered himself into the Riley. Eileen having seen the people was suddenly silent.

Johnno said, "Listen, I'm sorry—I had to protect—" He began again. "She's my sister," he said lamely.

"Take her away," begged the oarsman.

So we took Eileen home. All the way she cried and told Johnno he had ruined her evening and told us both we were common louts.

CHAPTER EIGHT

Nothing much came of the fight that I can remember. Johnno told his father he had tripped over a root on the way home and of course Eileen had to corroborate it. I don't think either of our fathers ever heard the truth.

Life was fairly normal after this—a depressing round of school and homework with Moloney and our fathers picking at us constantly.

The first term was about half over when there were two happenings on a day I'll never forget.

By now it was mid-April and the nights were closing in; often they were still and cold. On one of these evenings I said at the dinner table, "Tomorrow Johnno and I are going for our Bronze Medallions." I hadn't mentioned Johnno's name at home for some time.

My mother glanced at me quickly. "It's very late to swim, isn't it?"

"Well, we did the land drill and the duck-diving last month," I said, "but then the examiner was called away and he hasn't been able to come back till now."

My father must have had a bad day that day. He said irritably, "I wish you would pay as much attention to your work as you do to swimming. What did Mr Moloney say about the problems you were doing last night?"

What he had actually said wouldn't have borne repeating. "He said I used the wrong method," I answered.

"In what way?"

"Does it matter just now?" asked my mother uneasily.

"It matters a great deal," said my father. "This year is a critical one. I know Charlie can do the work and Mr Moloney knows he can. Why he must concentrate on medallions, bronze or otherwise, instead of keeping up with his class, I don't know."

"But I promised I'd be Johnno's patient and he's to be mine."

"Johnno! Johnno! That's about the only name we hear. What do you suppose Fred Johnston will be doing next year?" Here it was again. "He'll be digging drains, or assisting the nightman, I'll warrant."

"George!" said my mother.

"He's going to run away," I said challengingly.

My father put down the carving knife. "Going to run away, eh?" He leant over the table. "And I suppose you're going with him?"

My mother said quickly, "Look, this is all very silly. What do you think it's like for me to prepare a meal—"

"Are you?" asked my father looking at me.

Grandfather, who had been staring angrily down at his hands, exclaimed suddenly, "In six days the Lor-rd made heaven and earth—six *days,* mark you. And this upstart declares that man made himself; made himself out o' monkeys—"

"Evolved, father," said my mother loudly.

"Evolved? Evolved? Very well then—who made the first monkey?" He was glaring challengingly at my mother. "Did the first monkey make itself?"

"I don't know," said my mother hopelessly. "I don't know. All I can say is this: if we don't settle to our dinner like human beings, I'm going to leave this table."

My father took up the carving knife grumpily and Grandfather muttered ". . . products of a-theism—" I remained silent for the rest of the meal, not mentioning Johnno or anything about the Bronze Medallion. Life was becoming intolerable.

During that night a strong wind arose from the northwest. When I got out of bed I saw the waves running at

53

an angle up the beach under a gloomy sky. Grandfather tapped the glass and growled that we'd be lucky if the roof stayed on the house that night.

Early in the afternoon the examiner arrived—a tall, hollow-cheeked man wrapped in an overcoat. As there were no other candidates Johnno and I drove alone with him to the beach. The sea was louder now and spray blew occasionally across the L of the pier.

"You're both strong swimmers?"

When Johnno didn't answer I said, "He's the best in the town."

The examiner looked at me bleakly. "But you, you still want to go on with it yourself?"

"Yes," I said.

There was good reason for this: Johnno was the perfect patient; when he filled his lungs with air he floated like an inflated beach toy. I knew that if he left school I might never get the opportunity of having him again.

"Very well; get undressed as quickly as you can."

The dressing shed was deserted and had about it a winter look. It smelt of undisturbed salt deposits, and outside the tea-tree creaked depressingly.

All this was lost on Johnno. He was so at home in the sea and so glad to be out of school that a cyclone would have meant nothing to him.

We put our sweaters on and went on to the beach, our legs stinging in the blown sand. There was no one to be seen except the examiner who was striding up and down the pier. We walked beside him to the end, our eyes watering in the wind, the water making sucking sounds under our feet.

"It's a very poor day indeed. You're sure you want to go on with it?"

"Yes sir," we said.

"All right, you know the twenty-yard mark— the third bollard on the L. You, Reeve, will swim to a point opposite it, then Johnston will carry out the first method of release followed by the first method of rescue."

"Yes sir."

We handed him our sweaters and climbed down on to the landing. The decking was awash and the waves made rushing, slapping sounds round the piles. All this Johnno hardly noticed. He filled his great chest and dived in and began swimming parallel to the L, his feet fluttering rhythmically. I glanced inland at the town as a man might glance if seeing it for the last time, then I dived after him.

The water felt cold enough to stop my heart. Below the surface the depths were silent and hostile, reaching far into darkness. I curved up to the light and saw Johnno well ahead, treading water patiently. The movement of waves was against us as strongly as I had ever felt it.

"First method of release," cried Johnno.

I lifted my arms in fair imitation of a drowning man and felt them grasped and twisted outward. He turned me on my back, put his hands over my ears and presently I was riding with my head on his chest, all sound shut out, my face clear of the water. Above us was a grey sky, its cloud racing. Under me I could feel Johnno's legs driving powerfully. I relaxed and breathed deeply in preparation for the return.

As we came to the landing the examiner shouted, "First method of release and first method of rescue, Reeve."

We swam back together into the oncoming sea and faced each other twenty yards out. Johnno held up his arms and I turned him on to his back. He was unsinkable; even if waves washed continually over his face, he said nothing. But one thing he couldn't do was control our direction. We ended our run ten feet from the landing.

"All right," shouted the examiner, "don't bother to go back to the landing, swim from where you are. Your turn, Johnston—second method of release, second method of rescue."

Each time Johnno's turn came he attempted to correct my drift, but correcting it completely was beyond him, so we moved slowly down the pier.

Gradually fatigue crept over me, so that I began carrying out each movement automatically, hardly aware sometimes whether Johnno was the patient or the rescuer.

Drifting the way we were, we were beginning to lose protection from the L. Through the corner of my eye I could see the waves coming, and at the last moment would lift Johnno's head and submerge my own.

"Johnston—fourth method of rescue."

With his mouth near my ear he shouted, "You okay?"

I heard my own voice answer, "Okay."

"Reeve—fourth method of rescue."

On the last lap I had illusions of relief. The waves seemed less aggressive and the tremendous ache at the back of my neck was easier. The idea came to me that I was not in the water, but lying in bed, vaguely dreaming.

I heard the examiner from a long way off say, "Good work. Back to the landing and get dressed."

The landing was no more than fifty yards away, but it seemed beyond reach.

Johnno struck across the lines of waves, his body rising on crests and falling into troughs like a ship. I started after him, but found myself drifting rapidly towards the pier. The idea came to me that it would help to rest awhile by holding one of the piles. I was letting myself drift towards them when I was picked up by a wave and saw I would strike a pile. I dived under the crest, but in a second my head struck hard. As I surfaced in the trough the swirl held me to the pile. Somewhere up above the examiner was shouting, but before I could hear his words the next wave drove me against the pile with a turning motion and I felt mussel shells cut the insides of my arms and legs. In the same instant the pier lifebelt dangled beside me. I lunged at it, pushing my shoulders through it. A third wave swung me again, but when it had gone the two above hauled me on to the rough planking of the pier.

"My God, boy, why didn't you call for help?"

I heard Johnno say then, "I thought you were just behind me."

I sat up and saw myriads of small cuts on my arms and legs, done as if with razor-blades. On my forehead a lump was rising.

"Do you feel equal to walking?"

"Yes," I said uncertainly.

"We'd better go, then—a storm is coming."

The wind was still from the north-west, but much stronger than before. In the south-west the sky was black, the black clouds advancing quickly. I began to walk between Johnno and the examiner, my body feeling strangely light.

We were about half-way down the pier when the wind suddenly dropped and the air was momentarily still, then it came roaring from the south-west, low cloud flying before it. Inland we saw the trees bend together and branches go flying through the air. The beach was hidden under swirling sand.

"We're for it!" shouted the examiner. "Johnston, run and get the clothes and come to my car."

We found his Baby Austin with its hood torn off, but as soon as Johnno came back we drove straight to our place and reached it as the rain began. The house was shaking as if it would fall to pieces, and Gyp was hiding under Grandfather's bed.

CHAPTER NINE

Nothing much was said to me that night. My mother swabbed my legs with iodine, fanning them with a piece of cardboard, thinking I suppose, that this would ease the stinging. It was impossible to go to bed on the veranda. Rain washed its full length and blew under the front door and dripped in several places through the ceiling.

All night the house shook and creaked as if trying to uproot itself from the cliffs. Once there was a tremendous crash as Squid's look-out tree fell into our garden.

Apart from the confusion outside, my mind was confused from the happenings of the day. At times the waves and wind and the thrashing of trees was like a weird continuation of the moments on the pile.

Sometimes when the wind eased momentarily I would hear water gurgling in the down-pipes and overflowing from the tank and the rope snapping on Grandfather's flagpole.

I was sleeping on a couch not far inside the door leading on to the veranda. The bedrooms opened off this central room and it seemed to me that every time I opened my eyes my father or mother was going to Ian to assure him he was safe.

Towards dawn I was sleeping fitfully when a gust of cold air woke me, and a splashing of rain. I sat up, but the door was closed and I was still in darkness. After a few seconds I heard, even above the storm, a bellow from Grandfather, "Ship ahoy! All hands on deck!" Then a testy cry from my father to my mother, "Isn't it enough to be perched on a cliff-top on a night like this without having to curb a maniac."

"Lower away!" yelled Grandfather. His voice was blown by the gale, but even the gale could not overcome it. "Strike away, men! Watch for survivors!"

My father tripped over something, cursed luridly and flung open the door. He had switched on the veranda light and out there I saw Grandfather in a deluge of rain, his hair and beard blown, his pyjamas almost torn off. Rain and wind swept into the room and the light suddenly went out.

"Ready to take over, sir!" yelled my father. Then I heard him cry, "My God, there is a vessel!"

Forgetting my hurts I leapt off the couch and ran outside. In the first grey light, lying on her side on what we called "the second sandbank", was a yacht, the waves rolling her horribly.

"Here," said my father, taking Grandfather's arm. "You must get inside."

"I don't desert the bridge!" shouted Grandfather, his face streaming.

"You, Charlie, get Sergeant Gouvane."

I left the two of them struggling beside the binnacle and began running in my pyjamas to the police station, my legs rubbed and stinging.

The rain and wind were in my back hurtling me towards the town, then through the town, the rain horizontal in the street lights, twigs and leaves flying through the empty streets. I pounded on Sergeant Gouvane's front door and immediately his light went on. When he came I had hardly breath enough to speak. He stood glowering at me, a great slab of a man looking somehow the more threatening in his pyjamas.

"What is it?"

"A wreck—" I said.

"Where?"

"Opposite 'Thermopylae'."

He took hold of my shoulder. "Is this some dream of the old man's?"

"No," I said. "I saw it myself—a big yacht."

"I'll be there in five minutes."

He turned inside and I began running again down to the bike-shop in Beach Street. Standing there in the rain I knocked on the wall of Johnno's bedroom beside his head. After a bit he pulled aside the curtain, then came tumbling out.

"What is it?"

"A wreck," I said.

I gave him the story and we started back, Johnno running on ahead since by now I was out of breath and the cuts on my legs were raw from my wet pyjamas. As I went through the main street I could hear the firebell blowing in the wind, pealing weirdly. It was nearing full day, but a day like midwinter rather than April.

Down on the beach the sea was heaving and sickly. Johnno shouted to me, "Her mast's gone!"

I hardly heard him for the din of waves and I had no breath to answer him.

The waves were breaking now right over her. Gouvane was already on the beach, my father too and a couple of other men. They were attempting to launch a boat to see if anyone was trapped aboard, but each time they pushed it out, the boat broached to. We could hear none of their words for the wind.

Johnno shouted in my ear, "We could get the reel."

The door of the lifesaving club was never locked. We went to it and came back one at either end of the reel.

Gouvane came over to us. "What d' you intend doing with that?"

Johnno said, "I could swim out."

Gouvane looked at my father who had joined us. "What do you say?"

"Hardly possible," said my father, frowning.

"Well, we're not doing any good with the boat and we can't just stand here. There could easily be someone still aboard."

Johnno waited for no more, but stripped off his pyjamas and stood while I fastened the belt round him. On the sandbank we heard a loud crashing as something broke loose inside the hull. Presently the yacht heaved onto her side and lay with her bottom to the beach.

Johnno ran to the edge, the line trailing behind him. He bounded in a few yards, then was thrown off his feet. I saw him next on a wave top, then he disappeared. The sea was running at an angle to the beach, not in regular lines, but in short, vicious waves, their directions constantly changing. I saw Johnno again about twenty yards out moving slowly across the general direction of the sea. On the beach the line was running through Gouvane's hands.

"I'm not sure that we should have done this!" shouted my father.

Gouvane ignored him. Johnno was out of sight again, but the line was moving steadily. About a hundred yards had gone out. Next time we saw him he rose up on a high wave just abeam of the yacht, his arms still going tirelessly. He turned then and struck behind the wreck.

We all stood waiting on the beach in the pelting rain. Dr Stuart was there now, an army greatcoat over his pyjamas.

"Who is it out there?" I heard him shout to my father.

"Young Fred Johnston."

"He'll be damn' lucky if he gets back."

For my part there was never any doubt of Johnno getting back. However else he died, I couldn't imagine it being by drowning.

I noticed then that Grandfather McDonald was on the beach, his pyjamas clinging to his lank old frame, his beard like wet seaweed. He had got away from my mother and had come down the cliff path alone.

"How on earth—" I heard my father begin.

He and Dr Stuart stood one on either side of the old man and led him to the doctor's car. I believe when they drove home to our place, Grandfather cursed the doctor all the way for his interference.

By this time Johnno was on his way back, moving quite fast, though often out of sight in troughs. Gouvane had taken over the winding of the reel; the rest of us stood shivering at the edge of the water. Wreckage was beginning to come in: a smashed chair, a lifebelt, even a saturated book of signals.

Johnno reached the beach about half an hour after he had started. He was still on his knees on the sand, leaning on his hands, his chest heaving, when Gouvane shouted to him, "Was there a sign of anyone?"

He shook his head. After a bit I heard him say, "There were two broken mooring ropes—"

"Are you sure of this?"

"Yes, sir."

"Could you see her registration?"

"No, but her name was *Isis*."

That really was all there was to the wreck of the *Isis*. By afternoon the beach was strewn with her wreckage for a mile or more, and half the town was there to see it. Rumours began spreading concerning Johnno's swim and two people he was supposed to have rescued. For the rest of the day he was saying in an embarrassed voice, "No, it's not true; no, no one; it's not true," and so on. I kept wishing for him that it had been true.

CHAPTER TEN

After these happenings Johnno came in for a good deal
of admiration—though not, of course, from Moloney.
I believe Johnno himself would sooner have passed one
of Moloney's Monday tests than have been praised for
his swim. As it was, even my father praised him. "But
the world demands application and perseverance as well
as courage," he added.

At home the wreck had serious repercussions.
Grandfather had become so wet and cold and so worn
out by his climb down the cliffs that next day my mother
had to call in Dr Stuart.

I heard Grandfather bawl out, "Who gave you
permission to set foot in my door? No Bones touches
me while I've breath in my body."

The doctor was a man with flaming red hair and

a flaming temper. He shouted back, "I won't have long to wait, then! G'day to you."

He picked up his bag and walked out of the room. Grandfather, panting a good deal, called to my mother, "Show him the door and bolt it behind him."

But it was no good. Dr Stuart had to come back next day. He and Grandfather muttered and growled at one another all through the examination. It turned out that Grandfather had to stay in bed and had to lie propped up. There were whispers of pneumonia.

The trouble then was to keep him in bed, especially when the wind rose and the old house began shaking. My mother and father divided the night between them, and before long they became tired and irritable.

My task was to sit with him in the evenings after school. There was something depressing about this. Winter was coming on and evening crept into the high-ceilinged bedroom very early. And often the sea added to my melancholy. The window opened just above my bed on the northern veranda, but from where he lay Grandfather could see no more than thick tea-tree.

Each evening when I came in he would ask how the sea was running and the direction of the wind and state of the tide and ask me to read the barometer. Sometimes when I turned back to him I would see him staring like Henry Hudson adrift in his boat, his eyes defiant but hopeless. In the kitchen his old clock would strike out the hour as if hurrying him away.

On some nights I was relieved by Mr Theo Matthias, Grandfather's old debating friend. After these visits Grandfather was usually over-excited and unable to sleep. Despite his shortness of breath he would try to discuss the origin of man and whether T. H. Huxley was a Christian. Mr Matthias would stride out well satisfied, stick in hand, beard pointing aggressively from one side to the other as he walked.

In the middle of this period I became involved in an affair with Squid which, according to my father, "publicly disgraced our family".

One morning I left later than usual for school. This was a Monday, the morning of one of Moloney's tests. Out on the road, as I began running towards the short cut, I heard Squid yell, "I'll give y' a dink."

He drew up with me on his new bike and I jumped on the bar.

"That'll save you being late," he said into my ear.

We were scarcely a hundred yards down the road when we got a puncture. He left the bike at the nearest house and came back to me.

"We'd better run," I said. But it was no good; Squid never hurried to school—his mother claimed it gave him constipation.

He drew up with me, his head bobbing below the level of my eyes.

"We're going t' be a bit late anyhow," he said composedly.

"It's test morning," I reminded him.

"Yeah," he replied staring straight ahead. "Yeah." He thought seriously about this. "We'll get somethink on the produc's of France, I bet."

I looked at him quickly, but his face was innocent.

"I didn't know the products of France last exam," I said.

"You'll know 'em for certain this time then."

I made a sickly, noncommittal sound.

"Square root is what gets me," he said with a touch of anxiety. "How d' y' do it again?"

"Listen," I answered quickly, "we'd better walk faster."

We had only reached the top of Benson's Hill about half a mile from the school. Across the bush we could see the building itself, a sight to clutch the heart. We were only entering the bush when the sound of the bell drifted up to us.

"There it goes," I exclaimed, breaking into a run. I realized then that it was better to come in ten minutes late with Squid than five minutes late without him. I dropped back.

Squid said casually, "Mr Moloney's giving the strap like a threshing machine these days, don't you reckon?"

"You don't get it much," I retorted. "I daresay your mother's told him about your freckles."

He looked hurt. "No," he said. "No, I just think things out carefully."

"You'd better start thinking now," I burst out.

He was silent for some time, walking slowly. He said then, "My stomach feels crook."

"Well?"

"I reckon I might double up with pain an' you might have t' help me back home."

I clutched at this idea quickly. "What about after that?"

"My mother would give you a note: 'Dear Mr Moloney, My son Birdwood was took bad with gastro-somethink an' Charlie Reeve had t' help him back home. I'm sure, Mr Moloney, you will excuse Charlie for his—his thoughtful—'"

"Would she do it?"

"If I asked her she would."

I could see no other course. "You'd better get doubled up," I said.

Instead he sat in a patch of grass and began to turn up onion weeds for Christmas puddings. "I don't see why we got t' hurry."

I stood undecidedly, waiting for him to do something. From where we were we could see Donnelly's paddock on the edge of the town. There I noticed something that was to change our whole day. Strung out in the paddock were the coloured vans of Perry's circus complete with elephant, horses, donkeys and a cage of lions.

I said nothing, but Squid saw me staring and got quickly to his feet. He gave a despairing cry. "That's

Perry Brothers. Look, y' can see their elephant—the one that turned a hundred an' two last time they was here."

He gazed at me distractedly. "I can't hardly believe it. They're not due till next month." He added threateningly, "I can't be took sick today. We better start running."

We started half-heartedly.

"You could fall over," I said. "I could help you to school—"

"No," he panted, "your ideas would only get a feller inter trouble."

Even at this stage we might have been spared—Moloney might have had mercy on us; we might even have got to the circus. Instead, fate came along in the form of a camel. It stood beside a sheoak, feeding on the branches. I caught Squid's arm.

"A camel."

"Where?"

"By the sheoak."

He stopped. "It's a dromedary."

"What's the difference anyhow?"

"It's got a saddle on, so it must be a dromedary. Listen, it's Perry Brothers' dromedary."

"Well, let's clear out before someone comes for it," I said.

"No," he answered. "No." He was reaching a Napoleonic decision. "What we do is take the dromedary

72

t' Perry Brothers' an' Perry Brothers will see old Moloney—"

"You can if you want to."

"What'll you do?"

I could find no answer to this. I felt like knocking his freckled face off his shoulders. I stood undecidedly while he strode towards the camel.

"I'll come, then," I said.

We reached the sheoak where the camel stood dribbling greenly, surveying us with contemptuous eyes. It was a moth-eaten animal and it stank. Squid picked up its nose-line.

"Now we get it to lie down. I saw how to do it at last year's circus. Then we ride it."

"I don't want to ride it," I exclaimed.

"Well, I'm going to—there's nothink to it."

I looked round wildly, hoping for a miracle.

"Hooshta!" cried Squid with authority. He said to me, "That's telling it to lie down in Arab."

The camel roared in our faces with a foul breath, its neck striking like a snake.

"We'd better leave it."

"They always grizzle. The circus man said they're never happy, not even when you're feeding them."

"Hooshta!"

It darted its head at us, baring yellow teeth.

"Listen, let's go home."

"Hooshta!"

The camel dropped reluctantly to its knees. Squid's face was shining triumphantly.

"I'm not going to ride it."

He ignored me. As the camel subsided he climbed into the double saddle. As he sat there, the expression on his face reminded me of Rudolph Valentino.

"See you at school," he said carelessly.

The camel was moving to get up. I ran over to it and leapt up behind him.

The affair of Perry's camel was talked of for years round Kananook. I was always named as the main culprit. The truth was that I was only held in the saddle by a kind of paralysis. Squid was full of wild cries. He put his school cap on backwards and had a dirty hand-kerchief caught under the peak of it as a neck-cloth. Sometimes he clapped his hand up as a shield to his eyes and stared into the distance. There wasn't much doubt about what lay in the distance for it was obvious that the camel intended heading for the town.

I don't know when it was that I realized all wasn't well with Squid. After we had been swinging like a pair of metronomes for ten minutes I said faintly, "It's going to take us through the main street! What are we going to do?"

We were by this time approaching the sign WELCOME TO KANANOOK A GOOD REXONA TOWN.

"I dunno," said Squid in a hollow voice.

"You what?"

74

"I don't feel well."

He tried to lean on the neck of the camel, but it was too far off to be of comfort to him.

"I thought we'd given up the idea of you being sick?

"I can't help it—I feel crook in the stummick."

"Well, what do we do?"

"Don't talk," he begged.

At that point in our journey we engaged with our first townsman. The Presbyterian minister appeared in his buggy. The horse was moving with a sort of side-step, its ears twitching and its nostrils agape. For a moment it stopped and shivered all over, then emitting a sound I'd never heard from a horse, it wheeled round and was gone. Behind it the buggy scarcely touched the ground and Mr Wetherby scarcely touched the seat.

I prodded Squid. "We've killed Mr Wetherby."

"I'm glad," he moaned.

"You've got to do something."

"I'm going to jump off."

"You can't leave me."

"Ah, shut up," he wailed.

In the paddock by the local dairy I caught sight of cows performing an unmatronly dance, hind legs in the air, tails streaming out behind. At that moment Squid half fell, half jumped off. Scarcely pausing in its stride the camel kicked him into the roadside grass.

Any idea I had of following him was cut short when I heard him scream, "I'm dead!"

Alone I looked down the main street. Already horses were rearing up and men were trying to quieten them. I huddled miserably behind the neck of the camel. Outside the Pier Hotel I saw old Charlie Rolls fall on his knees at the edge of the gutter and assume an attitude of prayer. Ahead of me, lining the centre of the road, were loaves of bread. The baker's cart, with its door open, was travelling fast about a furlong in front of me. The camel advanced relentlessly, only pausing at Sam Yick's to eat most of Sam's display of Jonathans.

This journey through the town was one of the most depressing events of my childhood. Several tradespeople began pursuing us on foot, and the camel, by some fearful instinct, headed towards the school—in fact, its last act was to eat the top off old Moloney's favourite liquidambar.

This brought everyone tumbling out of the class-rooms, while behind me were the ranks of the tradespeople. There were cries of, "Mr Moloney, Charlie Reeve has come to school on a camel."

Moloney burst out of his office and strode through the ranks, his face unbelievable.

"So you ride to school on a camel, Reeve? By heavens, when I've finished with you, you will stand in the stirrups for a week! Get off that animal immediately!"

My voice came from a long way off. "It kicks, sir."

"So shall I—get off."

I slid miserably to the ground. A murmur passed through the tradespeople. This heralded the arrival of my father from his office. I felt a moment of deepened shame, remembering his sleepless nights and the worry at home. I heard him exclaim, "What's the meaning of this?"

I waved my hand in the direction of the camel in a way intended to be explanatory.

My father said coldly, "Mr Moloney, I leave him to you. I shall see him myself tonight."

With that he turned and strode away, looking neither right nor left, as if he had been caught in the street in his underpants. I was frog-marched then through the ranks of spectators, Mr Moloney breathing viciously in my ear.

So ended the affair of the camel—except that Squid had a week off from school after "a most unfortunate fall which has quite upset him". By this time my belief in justice was dead.

CHAPTER ELEVEN

For days after the camel business I might as well have been in jail. No one at home spoke to me; I was ordered to chop wood enough for weeks ahead; I was not allowed over to Johnno's, even though Johnno had had nothing to do with the affair. It was of no use trying to shift blame on to Squid. I had "misled him" and that was that. At school old Moloney did all he could to embarrass me. We were studying Arabia so he made a point of asking me for authoritative opinions on the use of camels and the life of Bedouins.

At home it was Grandfather who eventually had me reinstated. One afternoon when I came in from school he was feeling slightly better and asked for someone to read to him.

"You had better go in and make yourself useful," said my mother coldly.

I stepped into the dim room, nearly tripping over Gyp who had crept in and was studying Grandfather mournfully. Grandfather himself reminded me more than ever of the picture of Hudson adrift in the Arctic. His beard and hands were on the turned-down sheet, his hands fidgeting impatiently. He was muttering truculently to himself and eyed me sourly.

When he spoke there was more of a burr to his speech than I had ever heard.

"There's nae much that a man forced t' lie in his bed kin find consolation in," he said aloud. "Forced!" he repeated, glaring at me.

I stood there uneasily, saying nothing.

"Does she suppose I'm just goin' t' lie here?"

"Who?" I asked.

"Your mother—who else? Does she propose that I lie here till the breath has gone out o' me?"

"Of course not," I said quickly.

"'O' course not,' ye say, but I'm damn' sure that's what she's aboot. Listen"—he pinned me with his eye—"let non' of ye imagine that when God calls me I'll be lyin' in bed."

I did not know what to answer to this. I stood there fidgeting while he held me at the rapier point of his eye. "What could I read?" I asked.

He didn't answer me, but began a muttering tirade from which I could only pick up my mother's name and Dr Stuart's and the words "slow poison"—this addressed to his medicine bottles, which were kept out of his reach in case he hurled them through the window.

After a few minutes he seemed to remember why I was there.

"Read to me from the scrapbook," he ordered.

This was a book of newspaper clippings covering the wrecks that had occurred during his years in the pilot service. I had looked through it in the days before I could read, and even then had found that it cast a frightening spell over me. There were photographs of ships disappearing under the waves and others of four-masters like the *Holyhead* helpless on the rocks. When I had first begun reading as a child a vision of the Rip had formed in my mind—a kind of hell of waters swirling over drowned men. I had never quite lost the picture; in fact, I had only to read of the *Cheviot*, for instance— about her back breaking and the people trapped as her bows sank—for this picture to come back to me.

So I read from the scrapbook to Grandfather while the room grew darker. Outside the wind was rising and the sound of the sea was coming in at the open window.

"Read aboot the *Alert*."

This was another that had haunted me: the storm and the attempts to launch the Queenscliff lifeboat and the failure to save more than one man of fourteen.

I was reading about it when my mother came in with his tea. Grandfather looked at the plate and exclaimed, "Pap—nothing but damned pap!"

I left my mother trying to persuade him to eat it and went into the living-room to light the fire.

I was spoken to more favourably that night. It was a Monday again and not only had I read to Grandfather, I had also passed old Moloney's test for the first time.

We ate when Grandfather had been settled, but in the middle of the meal there was a shout from him. My mother and father hurried to his room. He declared he was sailing through the Rip and could make no progress; the ship was drifting towards the Corsair Rock.

They quietened him and came back to the table.

"I don't know how long this can go on," said my father frowning at his plate.

My mother said tiredly, "There's nothing more I can do."

A few days after this Grandfather took a turn for the worse and they had to begin all-night watches again. At six in the morning I would be called in and while dawn crawled to the windows I would sit listening in the cold to his quick breathing, feeling more alone than if I had been in the middle of the bush. On one of these mornings I became aware in the half light that he was watching me.

"And what d' they teach ye at school aboot evolution?" he demanded.

"Not much," I answered evasively.

"But what?"

I saw there was no avoiding the subject. "That we had the same ancestors as the apes—" I began.

"Moloney teaches ye this?"

"Not that we are descended from apes," I said. "Only that we had the same—"

But he was taking no notice of me. "What could ye expect from a man whose father was a bog-struttin' Irish peasant . . . ." His sentence ended in mutterings. I could only recognize the words, ". . . better that Darwin'd had a mill-stone roon' his neck an' been drooned i' the depths o' the sea."

In a few moments he was breathing heavily again and loneliness returned to me. An hour later I heard my mother get up and begin breaking sticks for the fire and filling kettles and setting the table. Presently there would be warmth in the kitchen and I could sit at the stove holding the toasting fork.

"There was the *Alert*," said Grandfather suddenly.

I said nothing, not knowing whether he was awake, or talking in his sleep.

"Ye hear me?"

"Yes," I said. "The *Alert*—"

"If they could ha' launched the Queenscliff boat, they'd ha' saved them, but in that sea there was nae hope."

My mother came in with a cup of tea. She said quietly, "That was a great help. You had better get ready for school."

As Grandfather deteriorated he became more and more determined to get out of bed, and it was almost impossible between the three of us to keep watch over him. At about this time Aunt Ruby turned up. Perhaps I should say who she was and why she had been the centre of family wrangling. She was the widow of my mother's eldest brother; in fact, my father always declared she had killed Uncle Bert through neglect. She would have countered this by shaking her head sorrowfully and declaring that poor dear Bert had lacked the faith to make him whole. My father would blow up when this was said and Aunt Ruby would release cascades of tears. No one could turn on tears or hysterics more rapidly than she could.

She was a short, plump woman with golden hair—rather tarnished-looking—and a pale face. She had protuberant eyes which went well with her capacity for pushing herself into other people's affairs.

As widow of the eldest son, she expected to inherit "Thermopylae" and was always ingratiating with "Pops" as she called Grandfather—a terrible name for a retired sea captain.

Probably because my mother was tired after weeks of watching over Grandfather, she more or less

83

welcomed Aunt Ruby. It was the first time I had seen her readily accepted. She stood at the back door with a bulging dress-basket in one hand and an umbrella in the other. Gyp had her bailed up there and was barking ferociously, while she poked at him with the point of the umbrella. She poked at him with that "all-right-we'll-see-who's-boss-around-here" expression of hers. We all came out and called Gyp away. He slunk off around the veranda cursing and growling to himself, trying to tell us that Aunt Ruby was an old rogue.

"It's you, Ruby," exclaimed my mother. "This is a surprise!"

I heard my father mutter, "It's a damn' shock."

But the two women were kissing each other and Aunt Ruby was saying, "As soon as I knew poor dear Pops was low I thought, 'Dear Ellen will need help.' What a trying time it is for all of us—"

"How did you hear?" asked my father, taking no part in the enthusiasm.

"I have means," said Aunt Ruby, raising her eyes to heaven. "When my loved ones are in danger, it is communicated—"

"You still go in for that stuff?"

"George," said my mother quickly, "would you take Ruby's dress-basket to Ian's room? You might put a piece of wood on the fire when you go in; in fact, I'm almost out of wood—"

My father waited for no more. He took the dress-basket and went off disgustedly, as if he were about to throw it into the sea. For her part Aunt Ruby went straight to Grandfather's room and in a moment we could hear her sobbing loudly.

"Get that disgusting woman out of there," growled my father.

In a moment she came out herself, a handkerchief to her eyes.

"Poor dear Pops, he's not to be long among us." She gave this as a fact that had been revealed to her. "Ellen, would you like me to watch during the night?"

My mother said that this was very kind of her—if she could watch until two it would be a great help.

Aunt Ruby installed herself in Ian's room as if the house were already hers. For his part Ian spent the evening whimpering and complaining that it wasn't fair. He was the smallest; he shouldn't have to share his room. He didn't like the way Aunt Ruby snored.

Aunt Ruby tousled his hair and said how sad it was that Providence hadn't blessed her with little ones.

I heard my father growl that Providence knew what it was about.

That night my father sat with Grandfather while we ate our tea. It spared him from having to share the table with Aunt Ruby. As far as she was concerned, she said a long grace, then had two helpings of everything, her pudgy, ring-weighted hands working at astonishing speed.

It was very cold that night with showers from the south. I was sleeping on the veranda still, directly under Grandfather's window. Around midnight I woke up, aware all at once that something was different, but unable to recognize what it was. After a moment I saw that Grandfather's light was on and that Aunt Ruby's shadow was on the blind. I fell asleep after this, the vague idea in my mind that Aunt Ruby and Grandfather were talking. In the morning I decided this could hardly have been so, as Grandfather was bad again and I had to get the doctor before we left for school.

A night or two after this my father had to go to a council meeting and for two or three hours my mother had to go out. Ian by this was in bed. Aunt Ruby said to me, "Don't sit up late, dear boy; you have had so much watching to do."

She looked at me with a mournful, heartfelt air. I didn't need much persuading to leave her. On the veranda there was not a sound from the sea. I lay awake for some time listening to the fishermen netting off the beach below the house.

I fancied as I went to sleep that Aunt Ruby came out and looked at me. My last thought was that perhaps she wasn't really a bad old girl after all.

Some time later Grandfather's voice woke me. I didn't hear what it was he said, but his voice was sharp and loud. His light was on again and Aunt Ruby's shadow was on the blind, huge and unmoving. I could hear her voice murmuring, but couldn't catch a word. Then I heard Grandfather speak sharply again, in an annoyed voice. I sat up in bed and looked at the window. It was shut top and bottom. While Aunt Ruby murmured again, I put my nails under and lifted it and quickly lay down. I saw her raise the curtain and peer into the darkness, wrinkling up her eyes. After a moment her voice came to me again, this time more clearly. She was standing close to Grandfather, trying to make him hear.

"Bert did a great deal for you. He said to me, 'Go to Pops when you need help. Pops will never see you wanting'."

There was no reply from the bed, but faintly I could hear Grandfather's harsh breathing.

"It's so little for you to do now, so little—" She broke off and I could hear her weeping. "I'm alone; unloved. For years I have turned the other cheek—" Her voice was broken by sobs, but gradually she calmed herself and said in a careful voice, "Pops, dear, it would only need your signature. If I helped you, you could write it, I'm sure. Think what it would mean!"

"No!" came Grandfather's voice. It was loud and indignant but produced with enormous effort.

"Dear Pops . . . . do you remember when you used to discuss the great biblical truths with me—the Garden, the coming of the Serpent—"

87

On it went without any reply. "There's the pen now," she said suddenly. "I'm sure the silent witnesses about us will smile—"

"No!" cried the voice again, so loudly this time that I was on my feet and in at the front door before I had thought what I was about. Aunt Ruby heard me coming and met me with an expression that frightened me.

"Well?" she demanded.

"What are you doing to Grandfather?"

She smiled sweetly all at once and whispered, "The poor dear has been restless. Did he wake you?"

"He was angry."

"Dear boy, you don't understand—his poor mind is wandering—"

"But you kept speaking to him."

"I?" she said sharply. "What did I say?"

Her eyes seemed to protrude more than ever.

"I don't know," I lied. "I just heard your voice."

Her expression eased. She said, "I comforted him once or twice, poor dear." She glanced gravely towards the bed. "He's asleep again. You go back to bed. It has all been a great strain for you, I know."

"I'm not going," I heard myself say.

"Not going?" she repeated, surprised.

"No," I said.

"You need your rest before you watch over Pops in the morning." Her expression was still pleasant and her voice full of consideration. "If he speaks again, don't let it trouble you."

I said stubbornly, "I want to stay with him."

"Oh?" she said. "Oh? I think you should do as I tell you."

Her face was flushing now, the flush spreading upward from her neck. She moved closer to me and for a moment I felt like giving in. Then Grandfather said something and she turned quickly back to him saying, "I'm here, dear Pops."

Without opening his eyes he muttered, "Get oot, woman."

Aunt Ruby turned and looked at me. "He's wandering, poor dear."

"I'm going to stay," I repeated.

She came quickly over to me. "Go out," she suddenly ordered. "Go back to bed."

Her voice was nothing like her ordinary voice and her expression had changed so much that I backed a few steps and came up against the wall.

"No," I said.

I was looking at her, half frightened, half fascinated, held by her eyes, which were bulging and furious. "Go out," she ordered hoarsely.

But even as I watched her, her expression suddenly changed and I thought she had had one of her visions. I swung round and saw my father at the door.

"All right, Ruby," he said in a level voice, "pack

your bag and get out." His face was like rock. Before him she seemed to shrivel up, and all at once she began weeping, not quietly, but with loud sobs.

"Charlie," said my father, "go back to bed. I'll call you at six."

So I went out, relieved to be out of the way. In a few minutes I heard raised voices, then Aunt Ruby screaming abuse and my father replying in the same level tones, his voice cold and furious. At the same time Gyp began barking under the veranda, and at last the door slammed and there was silence. My father came out and said, "You did very well." He paused a moment, then added, "Good night, old son."

"Good night," I said.

CHAPTER TWELVE

After the camel affair I had avoided Squid. For his part he sometimes glanced at me with an expression of hurt guilt, but we hardly exchanged a word.

Then, on the Saturday afternoon following the Aunt Ruby upset, his mother came to our back door and asked if I could go to the pictures with him. Poor dear Birdie was upset; apparently Charlie had misunderstood him in some way. It would be a happy reconciliation if Charlie cared to use the extra ticket Mr Glossop had sent and come home afterwards, too, with Birdie for tea.

On the whole my father disapproved of the pictures. He claimed that they had put an end to things like the local brass band and family songs around the piano, besides which he could never understand what manner of people could, every week, sit staring at shadows on a screen.

But this picture was *The Gold Rush*, so he gave his permission. For my part a reconciliation seemed almost worthwhile.

Mr Glossop, the manager of the Palais, used to send one of Jonas's cabs for Mrs Peters, usually a horse cab, but sometimes one of the new Overlands or Whippets. It rather spoilt things for Squid on the day of *The Gold Rush* when only a horse cab turned up with Dan Weekly driving.

While the cab waited, the horse tossed its nosebag and Dan sat up in front looking gloomily into steady rain.

Mrs Peters came out at last under an umbrella. If it was possible for a woman of forty to make herself look like an actress of twenty-two, then that woman was Mrs Peters. She was a mass of beads and eye-shadow and permanent waves; there was even a change in her manner.

Stepping up at the back she said, "Very well, Dan, you may go."

Dan untied the nosebag without speaking and tossed it on the floor beside him.

"Let down the flap, boys," said Mrs Peters.

We undid the straps and let it down, shutting ourselves in half darkness with the smell of leather seats and kerosene from the lamp. The cab began swaying

and the wheels made their running sound over the
road; occasionally there was a scraping from the brake.
Through the little window by Dan's head I saw the
park go by in the rain, and the Mechanics' Hall and
the Church of England. We swung round Wheeler's
corner, Dan holding out his whip to signal the turn,
then we drew up outside the Palais where the stalls
queue was waiting at the ticket box, the boys leaning
against the window of Fry's sweets shop and against
the hoardings showing Charlie Chaplin with his cane
and baggy trousers.

"Birdie," said Mrs Peters, "pay the driver, please—
and tip him."

We stepped stylishly over the flowing gutter,
causing a few jeers from the loungers. Mrs Peters swept
on grandly, bestowing a smile on Mr Glossop, a man
with a skewed nose, and a few strands of brownish hair
pasted over his skull.

"You boys go to the dress circle," she said loudly.
"I must study the music."

Only the most important people sat in the dress
circle: the doctor's family and the bank manager's
and the solicitor's, people who bought whole boxes
of chocolates before the lights went out and who
nodded their heads gravely to one another. Most of
them had permanent bookings and sometimes didn't
bother to use their seats even though they had paid
for them.

In the foyer, very perplexed-looking, was Johnno. He was reading the advertisements for *The Gold Rush*.

"G' day," said Squid. "We're going t' the flicks, me an' Charlie."

"Listen," said Johnno anxiously, "I've got ninepence."

"You better come in, then," said Squid generously.

"My money's for a haircut. I was just going to the barber's when I saw this—" He waved his hand at the advertisements.

"I've only got threepence," I said. "You can have that if you like."

"No," said Squid, hesitating at the foot of the stairs. "No; I got a better idea. I can cut hair. What we do is you come t' our place after the flicks and I cut your hair down in the Den for nothink."

Johnno rubbed his hand over his head concernedly. "No," he said. "No. My old man might notice—"

"All right, then," said Squid indifferently. He started up the stairs. "It doesn't matter t' me. Come on, Charlie." He added over his shoulder, "We got clippers, too."

Johnno said all at once, "All right, then, all right; I'll do it."

I passed him my threepence and he bought an upstairs ticket. I doubt that this had been Squid's intention; I think he had expected Johnno to sit in the stalls.

We had scarcely sat down when the lights went out and the advertisements started: Rogers the ironmonger; Willox the saddler; Hayes the blacksmith—

The rain was loud on the iron roof, but after a time Mrs Peters came in and the noise was defeated by a charge up and down the keyboard. She settled to "The Entrance of the Gladiators", then "Colonel Bogey" and "Under the Double Eagle". Squid chewed in time to the music and stared at the screen as if all this were old stuff. The last slide was shown and then the spotlight shone on Mrs Peters as she bowed this way and that. We clapped loudly.

Straight away the news starts: Mr Bruce strutting about a paddock in Canberra; the two sides of the Sydney Harbour Bridge stretched towards each other; "Boy" Charlton breathing hard after a race—

"That's what I want to be," says Johnno, raising his voice above the music.

Then the serial. A man and a girl are struggling on the edge of a cliff. Who they are and how they got there, Johnno and I have no idea. Squid whispers hoarsely, "He's one of Fu Manchu's blokes an' she knows he's got the opium. The other bloke's crashed over the cliffs on t' the rocks—"

"Help! Help! Will no one help me?" begs the caption.

Mrs Peters's arms are going like Jack Dempsey's.

"Robert! Robert! Where are you?"

Robert gallops from somewhere on a white horse and leaps out of the saddle, gun in hand.

"He's the goody," says Squid. "Watch him lay inter the crook."

Mrs Peters whacks a few electrifying chords and Robert throws himself forward. At this the film breaks. Downstairs whistling and stamping start and shouts of "Put a penny in." The only light is the little one over the piano. We listen to "The Doll Dance" and "Nola" before the screen lights up again. Something is still wrong. Robert runs backwards from the cliffs, rises in the air and lands in the saddle. The horse disappears backwards off the screen—

At half-time Johnno said he didn't know if coming to the pictures had been a good idea after all. He wasn't expected in till six, but the haircut was a terrible risk.

Squid said carelessly, "My mother's learned me how to cut hair. There's nothink to it."

"You're sure?"

"'Course I'm sure."

The electric bell went to go inside, and the ice-cream and lolly boys took the wire trays from round their necks and carried them back to Fry's shop.

We watched the Coming Attractions, Johnno and I knowing very well we wouldn't see them, Squid sure of them. Then came the main feature. I doubt whether Johnno enjoyed *The Gold Rush* much. Even at the part where Charlie cooks his boots, he leant over and said to me, "You really think he can cut hair?"

I answered yes to keep him quiet, but I could feel him fidgeting beside me unhappily, getting more and more restless as the picture neared its end.

The Gold Rush suffered only one interruption—not a break in the film, but the noise of a struggle on the fire-escape steps.

"It's Sergeant Gouvane an' Big Simmons's mob," whispered Squid. Sure enough the door burst open and there in unreal daylight was Gouvane manhandling three of the town's larrikins. "They try to look in at the flicks," added Squid dispassionately.

For a few seconds their voices and the sounds of the struggle prevailed against Mrs Peters' music; but then the door slammed and we were back in Alaska.

This was near the end of the programme. When we went outside, Gouvane had the three men near Fry's shop and was taking notes. All wore old Oxford bags and sweaters. Big Simmons himself had a silk scarf, once white, knotted round his neck. His nose had been bleeding, but he had his hands on his hips and every so often he spat beside Gouvane's feet. There was something about him that always frightened me—his animal expression perhaps and the glance he turned on passers-by. He was called "Big" to distinguish him from "Little", his brother, who was no better than he was.

We had passed the group when I heard him shout, "Stop that one, copper!"

The punch must have missed. By the time we turned, Gouvane had his arm up his back and Big was yelling, "You bloody copper bastard!" almost in a scream.

"I reckon we better get home," said Squid anxiously. When we had turned the corner he added to Johnno, "Charlie's coming to our place for tea, but we'll have tons of time f' the haircut before mum comes in. She gets played out after the flicks—Mr Glossop'll give her a cuppa tea somewhere."

The rain had stopped and the clouds had gone. The air was very still and cold. We walked slowly up the main street, then up the Esplanade, rising higher above the sea. The water was calm and grey; the air nipped our ears.

Johnno said, "You reckon you really know how to do it?"

"Known f' years," said Squid easily. "There's nothink to it once you've learnt."

As we walked farther Johnno said gloomily, "I really stole my old man's money—he hasn't got much, either."

"Stole it?" said Squid. "That wasn't stealing. You saved the haircut money, so if you saved it, he wouldn't hardly reckon it wasn't yours."

"You don't know my old man," said Johnno darkly.

Squid admitted that at his place his mother believed in philosophy and trusted him to see the best thing to do.

Johnno and I were silent at this. The three of us went slowly up the hill past the park. Cheering and hooting came from the football ground, and the wet thump of a football. The prospect of the haircut was beginning to weigh heavily even on me. If Squid made a mess, Johnno would be half killed.

When we reached the house Squid led us underneath it into the Den and we waited there while he got the clippers. The Den was a rough sort of place with about six feet of head-room at its highest end, a sand floor and bag walls. A light-bulb glowed over a couple of old chairs and a table. A bullock's head painted green was in one corner; in another was a drum marked POISEN. On a nail hung an A.I.F. hat complete with authentic bullet holes.

Squid came back with the clippers and a towel. "What style d' y' want it done?"

"Oh hell!" Johnno burst out. "Do it the same way it's always done."

Squid pulled one of the decrepit chairs under the light and waved Johnno into it. Johnno glanced at us as if he were a victim for electrocution. He sank into it and Squid tucked in the towel.

"Been wet, don't you reckon, sir?"

"For gawd's sake just hurry!" begged Johnno.

He had his head bowed and Squid was ploughing an experimental furrow. Certainly he seemed to have the art, even to the flourishes of the clippers. "Nothink to it," he murmured.

It was when he went over the furrow a second time that my heart faltered. It was so deep now that I knew there would be no way of fixing it. It was no use saying anything. I sank into a chair and looked at the ground between my feet, hardly able to bear what was happening.

I don't think Squid realized what he had done till three or four furrows lay side by side and a heap of ginger hair was scattered on the ground.

"Trouble is," he said, standing back, "trouble is you've had it the wrong style before."

"Just leave it the way it was," said Johnno distractedly.

It was too late for this. Squid began examining Johnno's head more frequently. After each examination he gave a clip here and a clip there. Johnno was beginning to look like a parrot with a large crest.

"Well," said Squid a little uneasily, "I reckon a bit off the front will about fix it."

He took out the scissors and clicked them a few times in the air and held the comb with one finger nicely raised. I turned away again and looked at the bag walls and began wishing we had never met Johnno at all. Next time I looked I could hardly believe it was

Johnno's head. Squid had fixed it, all right. In fact he himself was standing back with his mouth open.

"Is it finished?"

"Well," said Squid, recovering himself, "it needs a sort of—smoothing over, that's about all."

Johnno ran his hand over it. "Oh gawd," he cried, "it's all up and down!" He turned to me desperately. "Charlie, it's hacked about, isn't it?"

I felt half sick for him. "A bit," I admitted, "but not too bad—"

"Will my old man notice it?"

"No," said Squid hurriedly.

"But Charlie, do *you* reckon he'll notice it?"

I was casting about for an answer when we heard Mrs Peters coming into the house. Squid said urgently, "We better go up and you better go, Johnno."

"I'm clearing out, all right," said Johnno, feeling his head again. "I—I don't know what the hell to do."

From upstairs Mrs Peters cried, "Bird-ie."

"Just getting the wood," yelled Squid.

Outside it was dusk and fog was rising over the sea. Through the trees I could see the lights at "Thermopylae", yellow-looking in the damp air.

"I'll be late home, too," said Johnno hoarsely.

"It's only a quarter to six," I told him.

"Ah, well," he said resignedly. "So long."

"So long," I said.

But Squid said nothing.

101

"Well, it's a pleasure to have you," said Mrs Peters when we had gone inside. She was looking less like a film actress now. "I often tell Birdie how nice it is that he has such a friend next door." Squid was concentrating on the contents of various paper bags his mother had brought home. "And how is poor old Captain McDonald?"

"The doctor says he's a lot better," I told her.

"A dear old man. They don't make them like that any more. My old father was the same. Kept his interlect till the end."

"What are we having for tea?" asked Squid.

"Toasted crumpets," said Mrs Peters.

"They give me indergestion," said Squid frowning. "Can I have that cold pie from last night?"

"Of course, dear."

We sat down presently under the large portrait of Lance-Corporal Peters who stared down with a determinedly mournful expression on the small gathering. It was definitely an advantage to have lost a father in the war, I thought.

"I suppose, Charlie, you'll remain at 'Thermopylae' while the Captain holds to life?"

With my mouth full of crumpet I supposed we would.

"Of course, one is lucky to get a tenant in one's own home during such an emergency period, isn't one?"

I agreed that one was. Mrs Peters sighed over the whole situation and lowered her mascara'd eyelids.

"Old age is so sad. That at least they were spared," she added, raising her eyes to the Lance-Corporal. "'At the going down of the sun and at the rising thereof—'"

"Any more pie?" asked Squid.

"Dear boy, I'm sorry," said Mrs Peters. "But I have a special treat for you if you can wait till Charlie and I have finished our crumpets."

Squid supposed aggrievedly that he could wait.

"Such a poor eater," said Mrs Peters. She returned quickly to the subject of our house. "The Harrises have your place?"

"Yes," I said, my mouth full of crumpet again.

"Of course, folk in a position such as theirs could pay comparatively little, one would suppose, in rent?"

I supposed not.

"When do we get the surprise?" asked Squid.

"Patience is a virtue—" began Mrs Peters.

She was interrupted by a knocking on the front door.

"Do excuse me a moment, boys. It might be Mr Glossop come to consult me on tonight's music."

But it wasn't Mr Glossop, it was my mother, a scarf round her head and her face white.

"Charlie," she said, looking past Mrs Peters, "it's Grandfather—he got out of bed and we don't know where he is."

As I stood up I could see through the open door into the fog. I don't remember any further words. In a moment we were outside under invisible dripping trees.

"I fell asleep; oh dear, I fell asleep."

"Where's dad?"

"Looking in the garden."

The garden was submerged, but the house itself stood above the fog looking like the ship Grandfather imagined it to be. Soon the tide would cover it altogether.

"I was afraid this would happen; that I would fall asleep—"

My father called from somewhere ahead, "It's getting worse. We'd better get Charlie to go for Gouvane. We need a number of men with torches. He can't be out long in this sort of weather."

I was starting up the side of the house to go for Gouvane when I thought suddenly of Gyp. I stopped and called him and began whistling.

"Listen now," called my father from the other side of the house.

I stood there and presently heard a scrambling up the cliff path. I shouted then, "The boatshed! He may be in the boatshed."

I turned back and we started down between the wet tea-tree, Gyp disappearing again before us.

My father stepped on to the sand ahead of me. I heard him say, "You may have to go for the doctor."

"Yes," I said.

I felt suddenly that the familiar world was forsaking us, the old sure world of Grandfather's "Thermopylae".

From ahead of me again my father called, "The door's open. He's been trying to pull the boat out." He was silent then, and I could only hear the lapping of the water. Then I heard him exclaim, "Good God!"

I stopped walking.

"Call Gyp."

I whistled to him and when he came I held him, glad to have him near me.

"Go up and get your mother, then go for Dr Stuart."

I knew then the way it was. "Yes," I said. So I climbed up the cliff path and helped my mother down, then went along the beach towards the town.

CHAPTER FOURTEEN

Ian was sent away till Grandfather's funeral was over.

An oppressive silence fell over the old house and everywhere I went I was conscious that Grandfather lay at the centre of it, lifeless yet still dominating. A succession of people came to "see him". They moved on soft feet about the house and spoke in whispers and some of the women came out of the mysterious bedroom dabbing their eyes.

Mrs Peters was one. "Ah, what dignity, Mrs Reeve! Somethink about him reminds one of the epistles of old. Has Charlie seen him?"

My mother said no, she didn't think it necessary.

I began to feel I was being protected from something a man would face. When an opportunity came I went in alone.

The experience shocked me. Everyone had said how peaceful Grandfather looked and how young and how you could see family resemblances in his features. But to me his body looked like something discarded, something to be got quickly out of the way. It wasn't him any more. I went down to the beach and sat by the boatshed for a long time before I went back inside.

The funeral was a relief, but even it could not be a normal funeral. For one thing Aunt Ruby came, but instead of coming into the house for the service she stood outside the gate weeping bitterly. My mother went out and asked her to come in, but between loud sobs she declared that she knew when she wasn't wanted.

I heard my father say, "If that woman will neither come in nor go, I'll set the dog on her."

Aunt Ruby was probably the only person Gyp might have bitten.

My mother whispered urgently, "You shall do nothing of the sort."

So Aunt Ruby was left there, her head bowed and her tears falling like rain. Once she cried aloud, "Neglected! neglected! Oh, my poor dear Pops!"

The service was conducted by the Reverend Mr Wetherby—that minister whose horse had shied at our camel. We all packed into the old pine lounge, causing the floors to squeak rebelliously. From Grandfather's bedroom drifted the heavy scent of flowers, but out through the open door the sun shone reassuringly on a calm sea.

Mr Wetherby was a colourless man. He wore pince-nez and everything he said he read. He read "I am the resurrection and the life"; he read "Man that is born of woman hath but a short time to live;" he read that Grandfather had come to Victoria as a small boy, that he had been twenty years a ships' master and twenty years in the pilot service. Turning himself to my mother he read "words of comfort" to her, all in a monotone.

Behind him I could see old Mr Matthias fidgeting impatiently. Finally, when Mr Wetherby had uttered his last amen, Mr Matthias said in a low, resonant voice, "True; but not enough. By no means enough. Here was a noble man, a noble and courageous man; a man not given to the petty bickerings of this age. He can be numbered among the generation of pioneers who now, alas, are falling from among us." I glanced at my father and at Mr Wetherby to see what they would do, but they hadn't moved. Mr Wetherby was looking in a surprised way over the top of his glasses; my father's eyes were cast down and he was biting his lower lip. The people must have thought the address pre-arranged, for they listened intently. Mr Matthias's sonorous voice filled the room and his beard protruded aggressively. "He was a man unafraid to express his opinions even when these were contrary to the opinions of those who happened to be in authority over him; a man who would not deign to live by the sweat of another's brow." There was an uneasy shuffling at this—after all, Theo Matthias was supposed to be a Bolshevik. "And now"—more quietly—"his voice is stilled. No more shall we see him looking seawards from this old home; no more will we hear him in debate. But it is your hope and it is my hope—as a Christian it is my hope, Mr Wetherby—that this is not the end."

At this moment the rapid striking of Grand-father's old clock interrupted him. Whether he intended continuing, I don't know. My father hastily said "Amen," and at this the people muttered "Amen," and the service was over.

CHAPTER FIFTEEN

When I went back to school even old Moloney regarded me as a person apart, as if I had brought with me the atmosphere of Grandfather McDonald's last hours. "A sad loss," he said, then avoided speaking to me for the rest of the day.

My own attention was taken from the past few days by the sight of Johnno. He sat alone and his head was clipped as close as a criminal's. I couldn't see him on his own until lunch-time. Then, when we had climbed the post-and-rail fence and had gone into the bush and were lying on the damp turf, I said to him, looking at his head, "Was that because of the haircut?"

He felt it gingerly. "Yes—the old man did it." He looked at me accusingly. "Hell, Charlie, you shouldn't have let Squid make it like he did!"

I turned away from him. "No, I shouldn't have," I admitted. "But what could I do? It was the first cut that did it. Then I didn't know what to say."

"It would have been worse but for Eileen. The old man was all for half killing me, but she got between us and calmed him down. Then he went and borrowed clippers and did this." He felt it again. "Old Moloney said he didn't want a convict sitting with the rest, so he put me alone. I was going to take it out on Squid, but he hardly moved away from the classroom all day."

After this mournful recital we ate our sandwiches moodily. It was a windy day and all the surrounding bushes swayed against a cold sky.

"There's something else," said Johnno, frowning.

I looked at him again.

"It's Eileen. She was pretty good to me. Afterwards she asked if I'd take her to another dance."

So this was it!

"After what you did last time?" I exclaimed.

"Well—she's sort of forgotten that—"

"You're not reckoning on asking me again?"

"Hell, Charlie, it was partly your fault I got into trouble with the old man! You told me Squid could cut hair—"

"Anyhow, you couldn't go looking like that."

He felt his head again. "Eileen reckons it'll grow well enough in a couple of weeks. Listen, Charlie, you wouldn't—"

111

"Anyhow, we've had a death in the family." I felt suddenly grateful to Grandfather. "I don't see that I could ask to go to a dance—especially when Grandfather didn't believe in them."

I could see he thought this was taking a mean advantage of him. He sat tugging absently at a tuft of grass. "Okay then," he murmured despondently. "Okay."

I began to feel sorry for him, but then the bell went and we got up and walked without a word back to school.

He took Eileen alone to the second dance. As it turned out this made a big difference to us. To start with, Johnno came back from the dance looking almost happy. Alone at lunch-time again I said, "Well, what was it like?"

"The supper wasn't as good as last time," he said.

"Yes—but did you dance?"

"I did the foxtrot with Eileen to start her off—" He paused as if there were more to mention.

"What else?"

"Nothing," he replied quickly. "Listen, what about boxing practice?"

"You didn't dance with anyone else, did you?"

"No," he said loudly, "of course I didn't. Listen, if we don't start soon it won't be worth having a practice."

Boxing practice had been going on for weeks, in fact, ever since the cold weather had begun. I looked at him closely. Unlike Squid, he couldn't lie successfully. I knew he was certainly lying now.

"All right," I said carelessly, "you have first go."

He took a cord from his pocket and tied my wrists behind my back. I said nothing while this was going on. I knew there was something he was ashamed to admit. Eileen had probably talked him into dancing with someone else.

"Right?"

"Right," I said indifferently.

He began punching at me, quickly but with pulled punches, while I dodged and ducked. I began to forget about the dance and only kept my eyes on his. The worried look wasn't in them any longer. He watched me from under his brows. Had he liked, he could have killed me, but his blows seldom hurt. We changed over and I bound his wrists. He stepped lightly, as if the ground were hot, and while I punched he rolled and bobbed so well that I scarcely landed a blow.

"You want to get in," he said. "You're fair enough at defence, but you've got to punch as if you want to kill a bloke." When I untied him he demonstrated with a straight left and a right hook.

"About the dance—" I began.

"You want to think you're punching old Moloney."

The second bell saved him from my questions.

It was not long after this that Johnno began cleaning his shoes and wearing a tie. But worst of all he made himself conspicuous by using hair oil on his newly grown hair. My suspicions were aroused again; but he would tell nothing—except that Eileen had said she should have a brother she could look at without feeling ashamed.

I was even more suspicious when I went to his place one Saturday afternoon. Old man Johnston was working at his tool-bench amongst a mess of bicycle parts. The bench itself was black with years of grease and his own hands were not much better. I avoided him and knocked at the back door. Eileen came out, smartly dressed, smelling sickly sweet.

"Why, it's Charlie!" she said, twirling her strands of beads and putting her head to one side.

I ignored this. "Is Fred home?"

"I thought he was going to your place," she said, opening her eyes wide.

"He's not there," I answered. "At least, he wasn't when I came away."

"Do have a look again. If he's not there, I don't know where he could be."

I caught her smiling slightly. I exclaimed, "Oh, you know where he is, all right! He's never been the same since he went to the dance with you."

She laughed in a high-pitched way. "Run along, Charlie boy, and have a look."

I glared at her, but before I could say anything she had walked inside, singing "Charmaine" and swinging her hips.

I went home in a temper. Johnno was nowhere to be seen. At the side of the house Ian was climbing the pepper-tree.

"You never take me anywhere," he said in a whining voice. "You always promise, but you never take me."

"Shut up," I said.

"I'll tell Dad you said 'shut up'."

"I don't care. Have you seen Fred Johnston?"

"I'm not going to tell you."

"If you don't I'll pull you out of that tree."

He climbed higher and supposed himself to be out of reach. "If you try, I'll spit on you."

I ran over to the tree and, leaping up, grabbed his foot. He came down on top of me, knocking me to the ground at the same time, screaming, "Charlie's broken me back," and writhing realistically.

My father rushed to the veranda rail with one of his study books in his hand. "What in the name of heaven have you done now?"

"He fell out of the tree," I panted.

"He pulled me by my foot till I fell—"

"Stand up, both of you."

Ian struggled to his feet, his hand on his back. "Shut up and I'll take you yabbying," I hissed.

"What was that?" demanded my father.

"I told him I was sorry."

"And so you should be. Clear out—I don't care where—just clear out!"

CHAPTER SIXTEEN

As I walked away from the house I found myself blaming Johnno for my boredom. It came into my mind to do something without him, something he would be sorry to miss. The trouble was I had no idea what it could be. I still had no worthwhile ideas by the time I had reached the Mechanics' Hall. A number of people were about the hall, passing in and out, while others stood in groups outside. I remembered then that it was polling day.

I leant for a time against the sandy bank outside the hall—the spot where Johnno and I had waited for the Riley to come back on the night of the dance.

In their own slow way, polling days were interesting. All the peculiar people we didn't see for months at a time came out like insects from under lifted stones.

There were those like the Misses Ferguson who never stopped chewing aspirin while they were among other people and always spoke from behind a handkerchief soaked in eucalyptus. And there was Mrs Rolls, an extremely proud woman who hardly ever came out because she was so ashamed of her husband's drinking. She had made him live in a tent in his own backyard for nearly ten years. She had once been a strong temperance worker, a singer of songs like—

> *"Lips that touch wine*
> *Shall never touch mine"*

and had married Charlie, so I had heard my father say, with the idea of reforming him.

At the Mechanics' door Mr Turnbull was handing out How to Vote cards for the party which I knew stood for authority and respectability and such other proper things. Stinger Wray's father was handing out cards for the working man and "social justice".

Mr Turnbull wore a heavy overcoat and a bowler hat and he cleared his throat a lot and looked down importantly from a great height. Mr Wray was hatless and wore a reversible rubber raincoat. His boots were dirty and from his face you could tell that he believed life had done him great wrongs.

It might have made the day a bit interesting if they had argued, but I was disappointed to see that they seemed on quite friendly terms. Most people took a card from each of them, as if they were going to vote for both sides. It was all peaceful and dull and the afternoon was dull and cold.

I sat there for about ten minutes and was moving to go away when down past the Church of England came Mr Matthias, rucksack on his back, fly-veil round his hat—though there were no flies because it was winter—beard thrust out, book under one arm, mackintosh tightly buttoned, big loose knot to his tie, steel-rimmed glasses through which he didn't see well. He walked quickly, muttering to himself, slashing at the roadside grass with his heavy stick.

I hadn't seen him since Grandfather's funeral; in fact he was hardly seen now about the town at all. The idea that he was a Bolshevik had spread further since a day some weeks earlier when he had got into a political argument in the main street with Mr Glossop of the Palais Theatre. Mr Glossop had called him an anarchist and a few other things. His landlady, Mrs Prendergast, turned him out soon after this. She told my mother that she refused to share her roof with an anti-Christ. It didn't matter how my mother tried to explain to her and protect the old man, he was put out and that was that.

I believe we might have taken him into Grandfather's old room, but overnight he disappeared. It was said he was living in a hut in the bush about four miles east of the town. Someone—Squid I think—had

118

spread the story that Bolsheviks had been seen carrying a big wireless transmitter through the bush and that Mr Matthias had daily conversations with Russia.

As he came to the hall the two men at the door held How to Vote cards out to him. He took them and tore them to pieces and threw them to the wind.

"Do you know what I think of compulsory voting?" he shouted.

Mr Turnbull said solemnly, "Every man is entitled to his view in this democratic land—"

"All I intend doing is rendering my card invalid."

"Think of your responsibilities," cried Mr Wray.

"Think," bellowed Mr Matthias. "All you think of is grievances."

Mr Wray turned his back angrily, but Mr Turnbull laid his hand on the old man's arm. "Now, Matthias—"

"*Mr* Matthias."

"Very well, very well." Mr Turnbull drew himself up, raising his chin so that he looked down on Mr Matthias. "I can tell you I'm proud of my right to vote; proud to be a citizen of that Empire on which the sun never—"

"Bosh!" declared Mr Matthias, striding into the hall.

What went on there I couldn't see, but there was the sound of raised voices and presently Mr Matthias came out with his stick over his shoulder as if he had demolished the place. He went down the road, his head

119

thrust forward short-sightedly, his stick cutting at the grass again.

I knew then what I would do: I would follow him.

It was not a pleasant thing to do, to follow Mr Matthias when he had been such a friend of my grandfather's. I don't know what could have induced me to do it. Perhaps it was the mystery of where he lived and the talk about the transmitter. And, of course, it was an opportunity to do something unusual independently of Johnno. Just the same, I should not have done it.

Up past old Moloney's he went and across the school ground, then over the fence and into the bush, taking the track to the Lone Pine. I hesitated near the school fence—it was late afternoon and the bush looked oddly forbidding—but then I went on quickly.

The light was weak, and underfoot the sand made no sound. I walked on, looking ahead for him, my skin tingling for no reason at all. Not till I was near the Spy Tree did I see him, fifty yards on, stick still swinging and back bent. Beyond this point I hardly knew the bush. A faint track led into it, marked by a tobacco tin jammed in the fork of a wattle. Among the trees I crept closer to him till I could hear him muttering. He put his stick over his shoulder, as if he had left the country of his enemies behind. Now he began walking slowly through thicker growth. The path along this part was marked sometimes by broken branches, sometimes by little piles of twigs, once by an old shirt-tail tied to a bush. Each of these signs he looked for, then went on. The track climbed to a high, open ridge. Stooped there I looked back and saw the Lone Pine two miles or more away, and, well ahead, the water of Western Port.

Mr Matthias was out of sight, going downhill, walking faster. The afternoon was all but over by this, and I began to see I would be late home. I came on him suddenly again, near a Cootamundra in full blossom where once there must have been a house. Only the Cootamundra and some fruit-trees were left, and part of a stone wall.

After about a mile we came to the hut, a rough erection of vertical boards with a corrugated-iron roof and sheets of corrugated iron arranged as a chimney. It was in a clearing, but on three sides the bush was close up to it. A small window looked the way we had come, and next to it was a door with some words painted across it. He unlatched the door and disappeared inside.

I felt sorry for him then, and foolish; after all, he was only Mr Matthias, my Grandfather's friend. But I walked round the clearing, just inside the cover of trees.

At one place were the beginnings of a vegetable garden and, near it, a small spring. While I stood there smoke began to rise from the chimney. The daylight was going quickly now, and I realized I would have to run most of the way home. I began moving carefully away when suddenly the earth snatched at me and I felt as if an axe had cut off my foot. I heard myself yelling and saw my foot in a rabbit trap. At the same time there was a shout from inside. I stamped on the spring and jumped clear and began running, hardly knowing which way I was going.

Behind me Mr Matthias yelled, "I know who you are. Get back to your police station," and much more in the same vein.

His shouting slowly died behind me while I pounded through undergrowth in semi-darkness, my foot feeling like a piece of meat. I ran until I could scarcely breathe.

How long it had been dark I had no idea. Now and then I saw stars through the criss-cross of branches, but on the ground I could see nothing. I tried to run again, but stumbled through a creek and fell on to the opposite bank. I realized then that I was well off the track. Around me was thick darkness which seemed to throb with my throbbing foot. Ahead the ground rose steadily, and when I went on I could make out Lone Pine against the sky. The panic that had made me run had gone, and I could only hobble slowly towards the lights of the town. Even from there it took me an hour to get to "Thermopylae".

"Your father's at Fred Johnston's place looking for you," said my mother coldly. "Where have you been?"

"I got caught in a rabbit trap," I said, leaning against the wall.

122

"That's something new, anyway. Where did this happen?"

'In the bush—I stepped right in it. I can hardly walk."

At that point my father came pounding in at the back door, his face set angrily.

"What is it this time?" he blazed.

My mother said, "He caught his foot—"

"He can tell me, can't he?"

I tried to open my mouth. What would have happened I don't know. At that moment Ian burst into the room crying, "Gyp's a Labrador all right—look what he's brung me!"

He held up one of Mrs Peters' Plymouth Rocks, one of those Squid had hypnotized.

"It's dying," exclaimed my mother in dismay.

Gyp pushed the back door open and stood grinning with satisfaction, knocking the wall rhythmically with his tail.

"Tie that mongrel up," said my father, hanging on to himself.

My mother plunged into the medicine cupboard and brought out a bottle of brandy. "We'll never hear the end of this."

She poured a spoonful and tried to drop it into the hen's beak, but the hen had its eyes fixed on eternity and wasn't going to turn back even for brandy.

Ian came in again from tying Gyp up. "He's a retriever, all right; he didn't even wet its feathers."

123

"Be quiet!" said my father. "The hen's dead. Did Mrs Peters see it?"

Ian looked grave. "I don't reckon she did. It squawked, but Gyp brung it quickly—right to my feet—"

"Did she come out?"

"No; she was inside washing up—I could see her through the window."

"Listen now; I don't want anything said about this to *anyone*, understand?" We nodded seriously. "We'll get rid of that mongrel." Ian began to weep silently. "Charlie, you get out there and dig a hole, a deep one, and do it quickly, bad foot or no bad foot."

"He didn't know he was wrong—" began Ian.

"Quiet! Dig it on the side away from Peters'."

I hobbled outside and, even with my injured foot, dug to the length of the shovel. The rest was like the burial of Sir John Moore. When I went inside, my foot had turned blue and the marks of the trap's jaws showed as little red prints above my toes.

"Lie on the floor," said my mother. She poured the usual iodine on it while I writhed about, biting my lip.

"I don't know how I'll get to school tomorrow," I moaned.

"Well, we haven't a car, have we? Nor even a jinker?"

"You may care for a camel," my father put in sarcastically.

"All right," said my mother, deciding on peace. "Let's hear no more about it. We can expect Mrs Peters in at any moment, and what are we going to say?"

But Mrs Peters didn't come, and by next day it was even decided we could keep Gyp.

CHAPTER SEVENTEEN

As it turned out, I was home for a week with orders to stay in bed, but to keep up school work and complete homework.

"I'll have Birdie Peters bring your books home."

Squid enjoyed this. He came in with every book out of my desk and a few notes I had wanted no one to see. The look of the pile and its schoolroom smell spoilt the peacefulness of the room.

"What's up with you?" asked Squid, looking concerned.

"Caught my foot in a rabbit trap," I said.

He nodded seriously. "Toes gawn?"

"No," I said, bringing my foot out of the covers.

He stood back from it doubtfully. "Jus' broke 'em?"

I shook my head. "Cuts and bruises, that's all."

"Been injected?"

"No," I said, feeling I had missed out on something.

He looked glum at this. "Trouble is lockjaw. Didn't no one tell you?"

"No," I admitted.

"Starts in y' face. Y' teeth jam shut; after a bit y' head bends back till y' end up practically in a circle. Bloke mum knew in Adelaide got buried in a round coffin after lockjaw."

"Not me," I said uneasily.

I began unwinding the bandage as if lockjaw were nothing. The foot looked impressive—black round the toes with a row of scabs across it, the whole thing shading off to blues and greens, and on top of all this the iodine. It smelt rather peculiar too. I looked up and saw Squid hanging over the end of the bed, his face going the same green as my ankle.

"What's up?"

He rolled his eyes and disappeared onto the floor with a crash.

My mother came in quickly. "Whatever have you done? Birdie's nice enough to come and see you and all you do is bully him." She stooped over him gently.

"I only showed him my foot."

When she heard this she sat him on the floor and put his head between his knees.

"Ian, bring the smelling-salts—quickly."

On the floor Squid was making noises like a puppy.

127

"Quickly!"

When Ian came in Gyp was close behind him, eager to join the game on the floor.

"Get that dog out."

Gyp saved further argument by licking Squid's face and bringing him round.

"It's me stummick," I heard him say weakly.

My mother half lifted him outside. "The air will help you."

"There now," I heard from the veranda. "Lean against that for a while."

That was the last I saw of Squid for some time. He was good enough to send in a message though that anyone not knowing how to do simultaneous equations by the following Monday was "in for it".

Johnno came next day. My mother said afterwards how nice it was to see a boy beginning to take pride in his appearance. "His trousers pressed and his boots cleaned. What did he do to his hair though?"

I could hardly talk about him. All the time he was in the house he avoided my eyes and spoke only of school.

"We've got a new teacher—Miss Beckenstall."

"Some name!" I said.

"She's good," said Johnno.

"Old?"

"About twenty-three, they reckon. Moloney doesn't take us for anything now; he's with the sixth grade."

A feeling of peace came over me.

"She's given me two 'excellents' for compositions. Moloney would hardly give me ten out of twenty. She's a wake-up to Squid, too—keeps him in if he's late."

Perhaps after all there was going to be a reign of justice.

I didn't see Johnno again till the next Saturday evening. I was up by then. I limped to Mayfield's to get the *Sporting Globe,* and there was Johnno outside the shop, behaving very queerly. Once or twice he nearly went in, but at the last minute he changed his mind and instead read the posters as if they were tremendously important. All they said was MAGPIES FAVOURED FOR PREMIERSHIP and SCULLIN ACCUSES BRUCE, but he must have studied them five times. Then he walked away, but at the last minute changed his mind and came back again, travelling sideways like a crab.

As I crossed the street he saw me and tried to behave naturally, but when he realized I was going into the shop he was hardly able to speak. He followed me in, walking close behind me. I saw then that Noreen Logan had taken a job there and was serving behind the counter. She had only left school at the end of the past year and now was all curves and lipstick and eye-shadow and looked about twenty.

Johnno followed me to the counter and picked up a paper and began to read it as if his life depended on it. Mr Mayfield, who was an elder in the Presbyterian church, said, "Lad, I don't like to see young fellows reading *Beckett's Budget*."

Johnno dropped it quickly. I doubt that it could have harmed him—he had been holding it upside down.

Noreen turned to us and arched her eyebrows.

"Yes please?" she said to Johnno.

Johnno motioned dumbly towards me.

"*Globe*," I said, deliberately omitting "please". I wanted to show the way I imagined girls should be managed.

She brought it to me and I said carelessly, "Can you change ten bob?"

She frowned—probably because she couldn't work out the change. Johnno said quickly, "I've got threepence. I owe it to you anyhow for that time at the pictures."

He fumbled in his pockets and managed to bring it out. How he had come by this much money was a mystery. He held it out to Noreen, looking like a dog that has brought back a stick.

"Thank you, Freddie," she said softly. Freddie!

Johnno's eyes hardly left her. I trod on his foot, but he didn't even notice. She leant her elbows on the newspapers and said, "Cold, don't you think?"

"Yes," said Johnno dumbly. It would have been the same had she said hot or windy or anything else. Another customer came in, but Noreen still leant there while Johnno gazed at her.

130

Mr Mayfield came from the library section and looked at us disapprovingly. "Noreen, a lady is waiting." Then to us he said, "All right, boys, time to leave."

"Yes," said Johnno vaguely, not attempting to move. I caught hold of his arm and led him out of the shop.

I said, "I guessed it must be something like this; something low and sissy."

He didn't even hear me. He punched me joyfully in the ribs and pranced along like a racehorse. "Don't you reckon she's beaut?"

"She's a drip," I said. "She was a drip even in the first grade."

"—and the dress she had on," said Johnno, staring straight ahead. "Reminds me of Norma Talmadge—"

"You're mad, Johnno," I said.

He still didn't hear me. I left him abruptly, but I don't think he even noticed me go. He was still prancing along and was nothing like the real Johnno.

I limped home in low spirits. Johnno's company was as good as gone.

CHAPTER EIGHTEEN

Whatever else was wrong, school had improved remarkably. While old Moloney thrashed the sixth grade, Miss Beckenstall had us read *David Copperfield* in a way that brought the book to life. We had been about halfway through it and until then it had been dull stuff read without pause or explanation. Miss Beckenstall gave us each a part: David for me, Mr Micawber for Squid, Steerforth for Johnno, and so on.

"I don't like being Steerforth," said Johnno. "Look what he's done to Little Emily."

I wasn't sure what he had done to Little Emily; in any case Little Emily was being read by Janet Baker, who had nothing to recommend her.

"A chap's really bad if he's tough on women," said Johnno, gazing into the distance.

I looked at his face. It seemed to be looking sillier every day.

I tried to be serious. "It depends who the woman is."

"Well, Little Emily now—"

"She's only in a book."

He hadn't heard me. "I'd drop Steerforth cold." He punched the air absent-mindedly.

There was no need for this—Steerforth was drowned next day. "He must have been a hell of a swimmer," said Johnno afterwards.

With Miss Beckenstall we cleared up simultaneous equations quickly. She taught them so well that I believed I had discovered the art for myself. One day she called Johnno and me in while she was alone in the room eating her lunch. She told us to sit down and kept us waiting a few moments while she folded her serviette.

I looked at her carefully for the first time. Her hair was fair and smooth and was drawn back the way Sappho wore it in the picture over the blackboard. Her eyes were grey, and quick to change expression. It struck me all at once that she was beautiful. Before that moment a woman's beauty had meant nothing to me. I gazed at her warmly. She glanced up and smiled faintly. I felt my face get hot and turned quickly to see if Johnno had noticed anything, but he was looking absently out of the window.

Miss Beckenstall finished folding her serviette and said in a friendly voice, "You know, I had heard that you boys didn't work well, but this is something I can scarcely believe. I am very pleased indeed with both of you. I want you to promise me one thing: if you haven't understood anything, or if you want help, always come to me."

I felt surprised at the keenness we suddenly showed.

"You both have quite a gift for self-expression. I want to encourage you in your composition writing to express yourselves as freely as possible. I'm sure we can catch up any lost ground in mathematics. You only need to believe in yourselves."

When we went outside Johnno said, "She's terrific. She looks a bit like Noreen—"

"No," I interrupted. "Hell no!"

He shook his head in a puzzled way. "You're queer about girls, all right."

I didn't answer this. I looked at all the others, yelling as they played kick-the-kick out in the school ground. None of them really knew Miss Beckenstall as I did.

After lunch Miss Beckenstall took poetry. Usually we recited together with Moloney standing in front like a conductor, his eyes darting round the room to catch those who didn't know the piece he had set.

> *"An' when the cheery camp-fire*
> *Ex-plores the bush with gleams—"*

134

"Sit up, Gale!"

"The camping grounds were crow-ded
With cara-vansa teams—"

"D'dah, d'dah, d'dah-dah," from someone behind who didn't know it.

"Out here, Benson. This is poetry, the finest expression of our language, and you slouch in your desk chewing!"

Miss Beckenstall was not at all like this. She told us she would read a poem called "Ulysses" which was in blank verse. Here was Ulysses living at home after his travels. Even though he was old he was longing to make one more journey.

"Now I want you to listen carefully."

At first it sounded strange; but later I began to see it all:

"The lights begin to twinkle from the rocks:
The long day wanes: the slow moon climbs: the deep
Moans round with many voices. Come, my friends,
'Tis not too late to seek a newer world.
Push off, and sitting well in order smite
The sounding furrows; for my purpose holds
To sail beyond the sunset, and the baths
Of all the western stars, until I die."

135

I saw the boat launched at evening below "Thermopylae" and Johnno and one or two others bending with me at the oars. In the bows, looking towards the setting sun, stood Miss Beckenstall . . . .

"That poetry was pretty good," said Johnno afterwards. "That part 'To strive, to seek, to find; but'—something or other."

We looked across the sea as we walked home, across to the faint coast on the other side of the bay. Over there somewhere were the Otways, one of those places where Johnno had said he would find a hiding place when he ran away. He hadn't mentioned running away for some weeks. Perhaps spring had dissuaded him.

Next day he said, "We haven't climbed Lone Pine for a while."

We walked to it through the bush and climbed without a word to the board seat at the top. As soon as we had settled there with the town spread below and all the country sunny to the horizon, Johnno pulled a piece of paper out of his pocket. He said, "Last night I wrote something—it's poetry. I'll read it—no, you'd better read it, but not out loud."

I leant round the trunk and took it from him. "What's it called?"

"It hasn't got a name. It's not even finished."

Through a lot of crossing-out I read,

"We stood alone beside the sea,
The girl with honey hair and me
And no one else at all to see
And wind and sea all blowing free—"

It went on like this for three or four more lines till they "came home for tea".

"Pretty good," I said.

"No, it's lousy," he replied. "I got stuck on 'ee' every time I wrote a line. I didn't know how to stop."

"'Honey hair' sounds messy," I admitted.

"Well," he said, looking a long way off, "that's what it's like—you know, like sun shining through honey."

"*What's* like honey?"

He didn't answer and I couldn't see him for the trunk.

"You're mad if you think that dumb Logan girl's got hair like that."

He said loudly, "If you weren't my mate I'd dump you fair out of the tree!"

"Mate?" I repeated bitterly. "I only see you at school."

"Well," he said sighing to himself. "I don't know—it's hard to talk about."

"Did you meet her at the dance?"

"Yes," he admitted from behind the trunk.

"You *danced* with her?"

137

"In a tap dance I tapped her and no one tapped me, so we had the whole dance."

I peered round the trunk at him. He looked ridiculous with his carefully brushed hair and his pimples with the tops shaved off and his huge hands.

"I'm sorry for you," I said.

"I don't want to talk," he replied.

We climbed down despondently and even Miss Beckenstall didn't cheer me.

During the rest of the week Johnno must have been thinking things over. On the Friday he said brightly, "What about walking to Coles Bay tomorrow?"

The suggestion reminded me of old times, but I answered casually, "Not a bad idea. What time?"

"About ten," he said. "We could take something to grill for lunch."

"Okay," I said. "Okay."

CHAPTER NINETEEN

Coles bay was about three miles along the coast. A track wound to it along the cliff-top shut in most of the way by dense tea-tree. Here and there through gaps you could look down on the sea, on clear days right to the bottom, to greenish sand and rocks. Once we had swum there, exploring outcrops of rock under the water in a silent world with the sea around like curtains. Near the bottom we had seen something move. The sand had begun to rise like slow smoke and we had shot up together.

"Do you reckon on swimming this time?"

It was September, the month we usually started again.

"Too cold yet," said Johnno.

"Well, if it's warm enough when we get to the bay we can go in without togs—there's never anyone around there."

"I don't know about that," said Johnno. "They say a lot of people walk that way now just to see the view."

We took no togs. The day was the first really warm one we had had. We took sausages with us, and up above the sea grilled them over a tea-tree fire. Stooped there we grew hotter and hotter.

The sea was making lapping sounds along the bottom of the cliffs and the sun shone brilliantly on its surface.

"I'm going for a swim anyhow," I said.

Johnno shook his head. "You should wait an hour after a meal—probably an hour and a half after a meal like this."

I looked at him. "You used to go in any time. When we raided Collins' orchard, you ate quinces with water up to your neck."

"I didn't know then," he answered evasively. "Not long after that I saw a girl dragged out, just up from the town. They were trying resuscitation, but she was the colour your foot was. She didn't come round and they said it was because she had gone in after a meal."

I found this hard to accept from Johnno, but when we lay on a sloping, grassy spot I felt too drowsy to care. Even without sitting up we could see beyond our feet on to the backs of gulls skimming above the water. Their cries came up to us mixed with the lapping sounds. Spring was coming all around us.

I was dozing there, dreaming that Miss Beckenstall

was reading to me, when Johnno said, "We'd better get going."

"You woke me up," I said irritably. "Anyhow, let's stay here."

"All right," he said, looking around uneasily. He remained sitting while I lay down and slipped back to dreaming. Presently Miss Beckenstall took up her position in the bows and the brown sailors hoisted the sail. Sitting with the sun behind her she began reading above the sound of the sea:

"It little profits that an idle king,
By this still hearth, among these barren crags . . . ."

She read slowly. The sailors worked around us without a word. Miss Beckenstall wore a biblical-looking garment, caught by some sort of ancient brooch at her shoulder.

"The lights begin to twinkle from the rocks:
The long day wanes: the slow moon climbs: the deep
Moans round—"

"What d' you know!" cried a female voice. "Fancy meeting you boys here!"

Miss Beckenstall disappeared into the sea and beside us stood Noreen Logan and a friend of hers, Kitty Bailey, a dumb willowy blonde who had left school about a year ago to work the cash register at the Continental café. The two of them stood in the sunshine in summer frocks, swaying their hips and swinging their beads and making sure their jazz garters were in view. All at once I felt strangled. I looked at Johnno, but he avoided my eye.

"We were just out strolling—such a div-ine day."

"So ser-lubrious," added Kitty.

Still I could find nothing to say. The sight of them, so confident, brought a paralysis over me.

"And what are you men doing?" asked Noreen, looking interestedly down on us.

"We've just had lunch," said Johnno hoarsely. "Sausages."

"Yum, yum! We should of come sooner, Kit."

Kit rolled her eyes. I burst out to Johnno, "I thought no one came here?"

"Well—" He waved his hand helplessly.

"Some people," said Noreen, "*some* people think they own the whole town—and everyone in it, too."

"You mean me?"

"No, no; not you, sweet boy. Kitty, lend me a cigarette, there's a dear."

Kitty produced a packet of Magpies and a box of matches and the two of them began puffing expertly, hand on hip. Johnno looked embarrassed.

"May we sit down? Gentlemen usually ask ladies to sit down, you know."

"Yes, yes," said Johnno quickly.

They held their skirts delicately and sank beside us. Kitty adopted me and Johnno and Noreen began talking in low voices; I remained silent, my face hot.

"The view here is simply gor-geous, don't you think?" Kitty looked at me over the tip of her cigarette.

"I suppose so," I said.

I smelt the sea and her perfume and the coming of spring, a blending that was pleasantly disturbing, despite my annoyance.

"Have you been for a swim?"

"No," I answered.

"I saw you swimming last year—you're terrifically fast, aren't you?"

"Not as fast as Johnno."

"Oh, Freddie's fast, isn't he? Just ask Noreen!"

I couldn't find an answer to this subtlety. I stared down at the ashes of our fire.

Kitty looked sadly out to sea. "You don't like girls, do you?"

"They're all right, I suppose."

She turned towards me so that her bobbed hair blew over her face. "Freddie does," she said.

"Does what?"

"Well, he likes Noreen." She butted her cigarette and took out a compact and began operating on her lips. I watched this repair work in a kind of trance.

"Kitty, pet," said Noreen, interrupting, "me and Fred think we might walk a little way; we want a tat-a-tat, don't we, Freddie?"

Freddie made an embarrassed sound in his throat.

"Do you and Charlie want to sit here, or will you toddle, too?"

"Oh," said Kitty, "we might sit a while, don't you think, Charlie? Perhaps we'll follow—but not too close, eh?" She smothered a giggle.

Noreen stood up and brushed her frock and turned to see if it had crushed.

"Oh, Freddie, I've left my handbag on the ground."

Freddie picked it up like Gyp picking up the morning paper. Then they went off together. I looked after them and saw Fred take her hand. Here was the worst mark of a sissy, and this was *Johnno* holding her hand!

"Hell!" I burst out.

"Pardon?" said Kitty.

I looked helplessly after Johnno.

"He's rather a pet, isn't he? So fond of Noreen, too."

I could find no words to answer this.

"A pet," Kitty went on. Casting down her lashes, she added, "And you're a bit nice, too."

I was out of my depth now, but I said determinedly, "When did Johnno work it out to come here?"

"Oh, I suppose Wednesday when he walked home with Nor."

"Walked home?"

"Nor was working back Wednesday night."

An underworld was opening around me and Johnno was part of it. No doubt Eileen was in it too, and the Mechanics' Hall was a gathering place where secret arrangements were entered into. It held an alarming sort of attraction and repulsion at the same time.

Kitty was sitting with her arms round her knees, gazing out to sea.

"Do you like Ruth Chatterton?"

"Ruth who?"

"*You* know—the fillum star, the one in *Sins of the Fathers.*"

She saved me from admitting my ignorance by beginning to rummage in her handbag. From among various scented articles she produced a folded page from a magazine. She blew powder off it and opened it carefully. A blonde girl stared at me with that same smouldering, underworld expression. There was something, too, about her hair-style and her shadowed eyelids . . . .

"She reminds me of someone," I admitted.

"Oh?" said Kitty interestedly. "Who could it be, now?"

I glanced up and she was regarding me from under darkened lids, her lips curved.

"She reminds me—of you."

"Oh, Charlie, you do say the sweetest things! You don't go round paying compliments to *every* girl you meet, do you?"

It struck me all at once that I must have known a great deal about girls without realizing it. I leant over and took her hand as I had seen Johnno take Noreen's. It was a scented, manicured little hand, unbelievably soft.

"Oh, Charlie," she murmured. She leant towards me, her scent suddenly enveloping me, her hair brushing my cheek. I saw her curved lips waiting. Then somewhere beyond them, intruding alarmingly, I saw a pair of male shoes half-hidden by dirty Oxford bags.

I shot to my feet and found myself facing Big Simmons. He stood with half-closed eyes, hands on hips, breathing quickly.

"Ron," breathed Kitty. "Oh, Ron!"

"Shut up!" cried Big. "A bloke oughta belt you, telling a feller all that dope. Who's this runt?"

"Ronnie, he doesn't mean a thing to me. We just happened to meet—"

"You were getting on pretty good—holding bloody hands—"

"He made me—"

"He did, eh? Clear out then while me and him have a little talk."

Kitty scrambled up and made off in the direction opposite to Johnno. As we looked after her a fearful silence fell over the place; the waves stopped lapping on the rocks, the trees became still, the seagulls disappeared. Big spat at my feet. "Who said y' could take my sheila out?"

"I didn't take her—"

"My bloody oath you took her!"

My voice came from a long way off. "I just happened to meet her."

I watched him with horrible fascination—his coppery stubble and sideboards, his grubby sweater and narrow eyes. "By hell, y'll pay for this!"

When I saw no hope of reprieve, a feeling of stubbornness swam up through my fears. He was standing above me on the slope in a position of advantage. I watched him take his hands unhurriedly off his hips. He was "Big" Simmons; he had no need to hurry.

I didn't wait for him to punch, but dived and caught him below the knees with my shoulder. I felt him shoot over me and crash into the grass. But then I did nothing more than scramble to the level ground and hesitate as if it had all been a practice with Johnno.

He picked himself up and charged up the slope, arms out from sides and face twisted. "Smart bastard!"

He drove a straight right that would have taken my head. I ducked under it and rolled away, bringing my eyes back to his. He came quickly again, swinging left and right. Most of the blows missed; the rest I took on my arms and back glancingly.

He pressed in closer. "Fight, y' windy little bastard!"

I swayed right as he came in and saw his face unguarded. I punched his nose with all my strength and saw blood gush suddenly over his lip and chin.

He let out a bellow and drove his knee into my groin. As I doubled up he jumped in and wrapped an arm round my head and began punching my face with his other hand, grunting with each blow. I reached blindly for his ankle and wrenched his foot off the ground but his fingers went into my eyes deeply. There was a white light and someone screamed. He let go then and I felt myself rolling through darkness. The sea, I thought. The cliff! But my head came hard against something and I lost consciousness.

CHAPTER TWENTY

I knew it was daylight still by the blur of light. The girl's voice said again, "Leave him; you've got to leave him, or we'll really be in for it."

Then Johnno's voice answered. "You can if you like."

"If you don't come I'll never speak to you again."

"You don't have to," he said. "You can clear out."

She shouted something at him and that was all I heard of her.

I tried to open my eyes, but gasped with pain. I heard Johnno say, "Charlie—are you okay, Charlie?"

"I can't see," I said.

"Who was it?"

"Big Simmons. He got his fingers in my eyes."

I heard an intake of breath. "It's all my fault," he said.

"Has Noreen gone?"

"Yes," said Johnno flatly.

I was sitting up, feeling about me.

"Can you walk?"

"I think so," I said.

But when I stood up I found it harder than I had expected. It was three miles back to the town. Even with Johnno guiding me I travelled slowly, stumbling and swaying along the track, my eyes scalding. Every few minutes Johnno asked in a worried voice, "Can you see yet?"

But I could hardly answer for the pain.

I asked once, "Where are we now?"

"Near the Esplanade," he said. "You can't tell?"

"No," I said.

"It's just about dark," he told me.

I tried to open my eyes again but it was useless.

"They may be better in a while," I said. But I didn't believe it.

After a long time we began descending towards the town. I wondered vaguely then what my father would say, but the pain drove any real anxiety out of me.

Johnno said, "I better take you to Dr Stuart's."

We were scarcely speaking by this, but every now and then I felt his grip tighten anxiously.

We were somewhere in the main street when he gripped me so hard that I stopped. Almost at once

I heard my father's voice exclaim, "Good God, what's happened?"

"A fight," I said, my voice all at once uncontrollable.

"Who—?"

"Ron Simmons."

"It's my fault," I heard Johnno say.

But my father didn't answer him. I felt his hand on my shoulder. "What has he done to your eyes?"

"Dug his fingers into them."

I heard my father catch his breath. "Can you see?"

"A bit," I said.

"Did you see it happen, Fred?"

"No—no," stammered Johnno.

"He found me," I said. My voice was too unsteady to say more.

"We'll go to the doctor's. Fred, run to our place and tell Mrs Reeve we'll be late. Better tell her what's happened—try not to make it too worrying for her."

"No, sir," said Johnno. I had never heard him call my father sir before.

I heard him go away, then I went on alone with my father, walking slowly.

"It's hurting badly?"

"Yes," I said.

He held on to my arm, telling me when we were coming to kerbs.

"It might hurt having them examined," he warned.

We came to the doctor's gate, then crunched slowly up the gravel path and rang the doorbell. I heard Mrs Stuart senior, a sour old woman, come to the door and exclaim, "Now look, Mr Reeve, doctor's at dinner. He has to eat like other people, you know."

"My boy's in a good deal of pain," said my father firmly.

"Fighting, by the look of it."

"I'm not asking for your diagnosis. Just show me to the waiting-room and get the doctor."

Before she could reply I heard Dr Stuart push back his chair in the dining-room and call out, "Is that you, Mr Reeve?"

"It is," said my father. "Sorry to disturb you."

"A fight, did I hear?"

"You certainly did," replied Mrs Stuart.

"That's quite enough," he said to his mother. I heard her go snorting away. "A fight with the elder Simmons larrikin, eh?"

"When did you hear?" demanded my father.

"He came in with a broken nose," said the doctor. My father began to exclaim something but the doctor interrupted, "Splendid blow—about time someone did it. What's the damage here?"

"My eyes," I said, lifting my head.

"Good lord! How did this happen?"

"Dug his fingers into them," said my father.

The doctor tilted my head back. "Dug them in all right. Pretty nasty kind of fight, eh?" He took my arm. "Come into the surgery and we'll see what's to be done."

He pressed me into a chair and tilted my head back. "This may hurt."

He tried to open my right eye and at that I felt my head spin. I began sliding off the chair back into unconsciousness . . . .

When I came round I was on the surgery table, a tremendous burning in my eyes. From behind a light the doctor was saying, "That's my advice, anyhow. I can give him something to ease the pain on the journey up. You haven't a car, have you?"

"No," said my father.

"How much would a hire car run into?"

"Three pounds, I dare say; but that's what we'll do."

"Lot of money, but I see nothing else for it. They'll probably keep him for a bit—unless there's somewhere near by where he could stay?"

"My mother's. She's in East Melbourne—I'll telephone her."

I put my hand over my eyes.

"Hurting, eh?"

"Yes," I said.

"We're sending you to the Eye and Ear Hospital so that they can have a look at you. Just a precaution." He began bandaging my eyes firmly.

"How much do we owe you?" asked my father.

"I'll send an account—"

"No," said my father, "I avoid accounts if I possibly can."

"All right, all right. Becoming an unfashionable practice these days, I can tell you."

So we went up to Melbourne by hire car. This took half my father's wages for the week.

CHAPTER TWENTY-ONE

My grandmother's house was in Victoria Parade. To go to it was to go to another country; not an unknown country, but a country vaguely familiar. This country, I knew, was England. It was protected from Australian heat and lack of respectability by old, thick walls and by my grandmother herself.

To go in you pulled a brass bell-pull and, somewhere within, a bell jingled faintly. When you stepped inside and the door closed, all sound of cable trams and brewery wagons and Chinese market-carts was reduced to rumblings and you knew it was not Melbourne, but London, that rumbled outside. It did not intrude, it knew its place; in this cosy world everything knew its place. There were shelves of books bought in London and walls hung with generations of family portraits;

there were marble mantels with glass-domed clocks, and hanging lustres that split the light into rainbows; there was coal in the grates, and in one corner rested a musical box.

The holiest place was the drawing-room. In there I had always been urged to sit up straight and not to speak unless spoken to. Fidgeting and interrupting were not done, not done, not done.

My grandmother still dominated this house. She lived there alone now, having outlived a couple of spinster daughters and a bachelor son. Sitting at the head of the table at family gatherings she reminded me of Queen Victoria, body erect, hair parted at the centre, expression not amused.

I was glad I could not see her sharp eyes this night with my father when we came from the hospital. She made a "tch-tch" sound as we stood at the door, but instead of shaking hands as she normally did she kissed me lightly above the bandage. This, I felt, was a rare concession.

My father said, "He may be here a fortnight, mater. Can you manage?"

"Of course I can manage."

I was led upstairs to the small bedroom over the Parade and told to get undressed. I felt my way to the bed and got in.

The throbbing had eased, but my eyes were bandaged firmly. I lay back listening to the far sad cry of paper-boys and the sound of the gripman throwing the lever to coast a tram downhill.

Outside, I thought, is London and downstairs is Queen Victoria. Her voice came faintly to me from her London parlour.

"You fought, too, my boy. A phase, you know; a phase—"

"It's the type of lout he fought with," said my father.

"Well, the standards in a young country, you know . . . ."

I heard my father come softly upstairs. He stood for a time without speaking, then asked quietly, "You awake still, son?"

"Yes," I said.

"I must go home in a few minutes." He sat on the end of the bed. "You were fortunate that no permanent damage was done."

"How long will my eyes be bandaged?"

"Three or four days; perhaps more."

I moved impatiently.

"You should think of consequences before you get yourself involved in larrikinism."

"I couldn't help it," I answered.

"Just what happened?"

I became silent. Since I couldn't see his expression it was not so difficult to remain silent.

"I can tell you this," he said. "I'm going to see Sergeant Gouvane when I get back. Whatever the cause was, I'm not going to stand for a lout trying to blind you. Now, what can I say at the police station?"

"I don't know," I answered uneasily.

"Don't know? That's absurd, surely? What caused the argument in the first place?"

"You don't have to do anything to start a fight with the Simmons."

"No," he said. "No; I grant you that. Was Fred Johnston with you?"

I tried to think how my answer might involve him, but my mind moved slowly.

"Well, was he?"

"No," I said. "He came afterwards, after Ron Simmons had gone—" I hesitated. "My eyes are beginning to hurt," I said.

"Gouvane will go to Simmons," my father persisted. "What story is he likely to hear there?"

I had convinced myself that I was in pain again.

"My eyes—"

"Now look, son, I'm going home and I'm going to the police station. Something has to be decided about this tonight. I don't want to find you've told only half the story. Did you say anything to annoy Ron Simmons?"

"No," I said. Even to my own ears my voice sounded uncertain.

"Did he simply walk up and hit you?"

"Just about," I said.

"Was anyone else there?"

I hesitated.

"Who was it?"

I felt my face redden.

"Not Fred Johnston?"

"No," I said.

"One of the Simmons girls?"

What made him ask this I didn't know, but at the word "girls" something about me made him suspicious.

"Some other girl?"

I left this unanswered too long.

"Who now?"

"Kitty Bailey," I heard myself say.

"I see." He got up and began walking up and down beside the bed. "You happened to come on them at a time that—uh—annoyed him?"

"No, it wasn't like that—"

"Well?"

"He thought I was—out with her."

He stopped walking. "And were you?"

"No—not exactly."

"'Not exactly'? What does that mean?"

"I was going for a walk and I just happened to meet her."

He sat slowly on the bed again. "What sort of a girl is she?"

"Stupid," I said.

An awkward silence fell over us. Outside I could hear a cart rattling by and someone laughing.

"I haven't spoken much to you about girls when I come to think of it." He cleared his throat. "Just what happened when you met this girl?"

"Nothing. We just talked—"

"About—?"

"About Ruth Chatterton."

"Ruth who?"

"Ruth Chatterton—the film actress."

"Oh, I see." He paused and for a while I could hear him breathing. "Nothing else happened? I mean . . . ." I waited to see what he meant, but he didn't say. "You know," he said suddenly, "or perhaps you don't know— girls, or girls of her type anyway, are dangerous?"

I couldn't think of anything to say.

"I don't blame you for being—interested. After all, you are reaching an age when—uh—" His voice wavered, but he recovered by asking, "What happened then?"

"Big Simmons came along and got mad."

"And the girl?"

"She ran away."

"Hm." He was silent, as if trying to think again of things he should tell me. From downstairs my grandmother called, "George, it's time you were leaving."

He answered her, then said, "When you get home we must have a talk." He sounded more cheerful. "I'm glad you've told me about it, anyway. What do you think now?" he asked frankly. "Will it help to see Gouvane?"

"It might get me into worse trouble with Simmons," I said.

"It might do that, too," he agreed. "All the same, I don't want to see him get away with it." He got up off the bed. "Well, my boy, I must be off. Don't worry about it now anyway."

During the night I dreamt I was on the grassy patch at Coles Bay again, Big Simmons's arm locked round my head, his fingers in my eyes. I woke bathed in sweat, startled by the blackness behind the bandage. Outside I could hear the milkman dipping milk into my grandmother's billy, then the sound of his horse moving to the next house. My eyes were throbbing, the throbbing speeded by my heart . . . .

A clock somewhere chimed seven. The sound of feet increased below the window and trams became more frequent; paper-boys called in morning voices. From downstairs I could smell bacon and eggs cooking. After a time I heard my grandmother coming upstairs with dishes clinking on a tray.

"And how did the Wild Colonial Boy sleep last night?" There was a touch of disapproval in her voice.

"Very well, thank you," I lied.

"Sit up now and I'll help you with your breakfast."

The bandage remained on for three days. By then I had learnt all the outside sounds, from the soft footfalls

161

of the Chinese vegetable man trotting with his pole over shoulder, to the trundle of brewery wagons down Victoria Parade.

Each day my grandmother took me by tram to the hospital. Because it was easiest to step on and off the dummy, we rode at the front, the swish of air on our faces and the sound of the gripman's levers behind us. I daresay we looked an odd pair: the erect, dignified old lady leading a shambling, blindfolded boy whose worn clothes were much too small for him.

When the bandage came off my grandmother said to me, "I think now you will be able to make the journey alone. It will be a pleasant walk for you."

I went to a mirror for the first time and found myself scarcely recognizable. My eyes were black and the eyeballs themselves were red; my hair had been combed forward in a peculiar Edwardian sort of way by my grandmother. Even though my reflection was blurred I saw, too, that I should commence shaving. Either I had forgotten how advanced my beard was or it had appeared in a matter of days. While I looked at myself my grandmother came into the room. She said, as if reading my thoughts, "I think you should perhaps use this—it was your grandfather's."

She handed me a cut-throat razor.

Two evenings later I was allowed to go alone into the city. I walked past St Pat's and down Bourke Street and through to Little Collins Street, past cobblers' and barbers', and hotels and chemists', each place with people at work or waiting there, each person seen a moment then gone, seen then gone. Past horses tossing nosebags while lorries were loaded, in and out of lighted arcades where there were tearooms and book-stalls. Unlike home, everyone was a stranger. There were men with lathered faces seen through barbers' windows, women trying on hats, men with raucous voices selling fruit, men and women brushing past hurrying to trams and trains. Lights were going on for late shopping.

I had turned into a long arcade when I saw a man and a woman looking into a jeweller's window at trays of engagement rings. The woman held the man's arm and with her other hand was pointing. Their heads were close together as they talked.

As I passed, the woman turned to the man exclaiming, "But really, darling—"

At the same moment I saw her face. It was Miss Beckenstall. I paused in mid-step, then walked on, my heart bumping. I hadn't seen the man's face, but I hated him and I hated Miss Beckenstall for having deceived me.

I glanced back down the arcade and saw them coming my way, noticing nothing but each other. They crossed the road, then stepped into a tram. I saw her for a moment in the golden interior. The gripman threw the lever and she was gone. Underground the cable hummed sadly to itself.

Before I went home a letter came from Eileen Johnston. "Dear Charlie, How all this happened I don't know and Fred won't tell me. All I know is he went to Simmons's place on his own on Sunday and came back with his clothes torn and his cheek cut. I tried to clean him up before Dad saw him, but I hadn't got finished when the police came. There was a fearful row with Dad and Sergeant Gouvane and Fred all locked in Dad's room. Your name was yelled a few times. I'm sure Fred went after Ron Simmons for fighting you, but both the Simmons set on him.

"I'm sorry about your eyes, but why did Fred have to pick a fight? Dad's got him home today. He says he can start work next week at 'Digger' Hayes', which is terrible . . . ." Digger Hayes was the blacksmith.

On the first day back at school I saw Johnno sitting in his usual place. He looked older and more than usually troubled, and there were dark stitches on his cheekbone. Miss Beckenstall began to write on the board. She took up the duster in her other hand and I saw that she was wearing an engagement ring. I knew then that all women— Miss Beckenstall, Eileen Johnston, Kitty Bailey, the whole lot of them—were full of deceit.

Johnno said at lunch-time, "Miss Beckenstall saw the old man."

"What did she tell him?"

"I don't know—I had to go outside. Anyhow, he's let me come back, but I'm working on Saturday mornings from now until the end of the year."

Almost without thinking we climbed over the bottom fence and walked into the bush towards Lone Pine. There on its hill it looked like an old friend who would never let us down.

"How are your eyes?"

"Just about right," I said. "They go blurry sometimes, but the doctor says they'll get better."

Johnno smiled to himself. "You made a mess of Big Simmons's nose."

I felt pleased. "It was the only time I hit him."

"You went to his place on purpose?" I asked him then.

He didn't explain his motives; he told the story briefly. "I hung about near the house and when Big came out I called him over. I saw his nose then—all taped up. He called to Little Simmons and Little yelled, 'I'll hold the bastard and you give it to him.' But with his nose the way it was Big wasn't game to come close till his brother could grab me, so I made sure I wasn't grabbed. That's about all."

"And Gouvane?"

"He came just after I'd knocked Little down and Big was coming in with a picket."

We had reached the tree by now. Our hands went to the usual branches and we climbed slowly. All the coast opened below us and the Dandenongs far off to the north. When we sat on the board Johnno said, "I'm done with girls. I'll never get married."

"Neither will I," I said.

CHAPTER TWENTY-TWO

When I look back, much of 1929 seems to have been taken up with outlandish happenings. Perhaps, though, my memory tends to exaggerate, or perhaps we turned small events into drama; I don't know. In actual fact there were long weeks at school when nothing much happened at all and then, after Johnno had been sent to the blacksmith's, there were dreary week-ends when I hardly knew what to do with myself. There was no let-up during these week-ends for Johnno. When Digger Hayes closed down at twelve o'clock on Saturdays, Johnno would have to start work at home, chopping wood or even scrubbing floors. I kept away from Navy Bike Repairs in case I caused him further trouble.

A few of us, though, would go to the smithy on Saturday mornings. Some went to commiserate with Johnno; others because they liked an excuse to be there.

It was a long, dark cave of a place where three men at a time worked on horses, stooping over their hoofs, cursing them, pulling out old nails and hammering in new ones. Half-finished spring-carts and jinkers stood at one end. Digger Hayes himself often worked on these, plus two or three other men, one of whom painted names and decorations on bakers' and butchers' carts. At the end was the grimiest office in the town—cobwebbed windows, papers stuck on nails, horseshoes holding down piles of accounts, swallows' nests in the rafters. About the whole place was a smell of singed hoofs and horse-dung and the coke fire. At first I envied Johnno working there, but as the weather became warmer I began to feel sorry for him and had little idea what to do without him.

One Saturday morning late in October I dropped in to see him at about ten o'clock. He was swinging a sledgehammer, beating a length of red-hot iron while Digger Hayes held it this way and that and came in himself with a smaller hammer, beating with quick, short strokes, ringing his hammer on the anvil.

"All right, young Reeve, on to the bloody bellows."

Digger was a man to obey. As I pulled the bellows I saw Windy Gale come in and Fat Benson and one or two others.

"Right, Windy-bloody-Gale, pick up a few horse-shoes."

Then Squid came, but he remained far enough back to avoid work. Sick of pulling the bellows, I changed with Fat and went over to where Squid leant at the door.

"G' day," he said. He looked at me from the corner of his eye and I knew that he had some idea in mind and that I must be on my guard.

After a few preliminaries he said, "Seen a good flick last night—about a bullfight." I showed no interest, but he pressed on. "This mat'dor bloke gets booed by the crowd, because they reckon he's windy. Even the senorita he's engaged to won't talk to him. So what does he do? There's a huge bull called Satan that no one ever has fought—bull 'bout as long as from here t' Johnno." This was about twenty feet. "So Satan's brought to the city an' everythink's ready f' the mat'dor bloke t' fight it. Then the senorita gets scared stiff an' runs t' his place an' flings herself at his feet and asks him not t' fight this bull, says she'll marry him straight off. Anyhow, he won't listen, so all she can do is give him the cross she wears next to her heart. Next thing it's the bull-ring—people everywhere, trumpets blowing. Into the ring comes blokes in tight pants and fancy jackets, all carrying darts, then blokes carrying spears and riding horses. Anyhow, in comes the bull, tossing his head, pawing the ground." Squid rubbed his feet realistically on the smithy floor. "One of the blokes with a dart throws it, then the game's on—darts everywhere an' spears an' the bull getting hostile, rushing round, knocking blokes down. Then in comes the mat'dor bloke with a sword. Up in the mob the senorita is busting out crying, covering her face with her fan." He paused at this stage.

"What happened next?"

"It's continued next week."

"Hell!" I exclaimed disgustedly.

"Anyhow," said Squid, "it give me an idea."

This was it. I had been caught enough by Squid's ideas; I didn't answer. Behind us in the smithy Johnno was swinging the hammer still and Fat was pulling the bellows. Horses stamped and whinnied.

"What I reckoned was we could have our own bullfight."

"I can tell you one feller who won't be there."

"Windy would," said Squid. "So would Fat 'n' a couple of others."

"You've got everything except a bull," I said scornfully.

"We got that, too."

"Where?"

"Up in the pound," he said guardedly. "Donnelly's big Hereford."

"It's older than old Donnelly himself."

"It'd be good to practise with, anyhow."

I said again, "Not for me—not even if you hypnotize it."

Squid turned away. "I could hypnotize it easy enough if I wanted to."

"Who's the matador?"

"Well, I'd reckoned you might want to be—not to kill the bull, I don't mean; if you just touch him on the neck you win—"

"What if he wins?"

"Anyone could get away from Donnelly's bull."

"You try it then!"

"I'm a pixador—with a spear."

"And a horse?"

"Well, there's a chance maybe I can borrer one."

"A camel may be better," I said.

Squid looked hurt at this.

"Okay," he said wearily. "Okay. If you don't want t' come I'll find another mat'dor. If Johnno wasn't working I know he'd be in it."

So we left it at that and I went back into the smithy and helped paint a spring-cart—which was not much of a job, but something to do.

By the time lunch was over I began thinking almost involuntarily of the bullfight; in fact, by three o'clock I found my legs moving towards the pound even before I realized I was going there.

The pound was on the eastern edge of the town. You passed the main shops, then the timber-yards, then the hay and corn store, then a house on its own belonging to

171

old Charlie Rolls and Mrs Rolls. Charlie Rolls lived on some sort of pension and spent most of his time at the Pier Hotel either inside or leaning by the door, depending on whether or not he had money. He was a sorry-looking man: turned-down walrus moustache, turned-down old hat, mournful eyes. His wife was a grim-looking woman. As I have said before, she had long ago kicked Charlie out of the house. His tent was in the backyard, on the edge of a few acres of unfenced bush. When he was drunk, all he wanted to do was sing to people, or tell them how he and Melba had filled the Melbourne Town Hall.

The pound was in a hollow a few hundred yards beyond the patch of bush. It was a pleasant green paddock with a tea-tree hedge on all except one side. This one side had a high four-bar fence, one of the first fences built in the town. Usually a horse or two was inside, or perhaps a cow, but I had never before seen a bull there.

My idea was to watch; I had no intention of letting Squid know I had come. I cut through Rolls' bush and came up to the pound behind one of the hedges.

As I approached I could hear voices clearly—Squid's and Windy Gale's and Fat Benson's and one or two others. The bottom of the hedge was very thick, but hollowed in places where boys had made hiding holes. I pushed into one of these and saw, only a few feet away, Donnelly's bull. It had its head down and was munching the grass, snorting peacefully. It was an ugly bull—reddish-looking eyes, a white face; matted, curly hair round its head. Its horns curved outwards to sharp points and the ring in its nose was worn from years of dragging on the grass.

Outside the post-and-rail fence Squid was organizing things. He was on an old horse with a drooping head; every rib of it was showing. Whose it was I had no idea. No saddle was on it, but from somewhere Squid had borrowed a bridle. He sat up like Napoleon directing his troops.

"Right now, the banderliras get first go. Got y' darts ready?"

They had made darts from lengths of swamp tea-tree about eighteen inches long—the sort of darts thrown with a string caught in a notch and wound round a finger.

Two banderilleros looked doubtfully at the rear of the bull.

Windy was one. He had a high, piping voice. "When d' *you* go in?" he asked Squid.

"Me? Well, this horse here belongs t' someone else an' I promised not t' get it excited, so I reckon it'd be best if I stuck the spear in from about here."

"Outside of the fence?"

"Well—maybe not."

There was a doubtful silence after this.

"If outside's good enough f' the pixador, it ought t' be good enough f' the banderliras," said Fat's mournful voice.

"In the flick—" began Squid.

"Yeah, but those blokes in the flicks," continued Fat, "they have other blokes t' do the tough things for 'm. Y'd never get Ramon Navarrer sticking—"

"I'll do it," broke in Windy contemptuously. "I reckoned I'd fight a bull, an' by hell that's what I'll do!"

He swaggered up to the fence and climbed on to it. It moved under him a little with age. He carried a piece of red flannelette with him and a handful of darts. The unsuspecting bull still munched and snorted contentedly, releasing an odour of chewed grass.

"C'mon, y' big yeller bastard," challenged Windy from the fence.

The bull didn't seem to care much about birth or courage.

"Needs t' see the red cloth, I'd reckon," said Squid.

Windy waved the cloth from the fence. The bull looked over its shoulder, but returned to the grass.

"How can y' have a bullfight if y've got a bull that won't fight?" asked Windy.

"In the flick," said Squid, "the blokes with the darts sort of pranced round where the bull could see 'em, then they let him have it in the neck."

Windy looked down doubtfully from the top rail of the fence.

"'Course," added Squid, "it'd take a bit o' guts with the savage bulls they got over there."

Windy apparently thought his reputation was at stake. He slid silently to the bull's side of the fence and stood there challengingly with his handful of darts. Even so, he looked as if he could hardly believe he was really there.

"Good on yer, Windy," breathed someone, "you'll do us."

Windy hitched up his pants and advanced cautiously. The bull, having finished a patch of capeweed, turned the other way and faced his challenger. Windy took a few steps back and glanced round to measure the height of the fence with his eye. The bull didn't stop eating. Windy began breathing again.

Outside on his charger the picador said casually, "I dunno—this bull ain't hardly worth fighting. Even a Spanish bloke couldn't get him in'rested."

Windy accepted this as a further challenge. He walked boldly towards the bull, at the same time preparing his first dart. He looped the knotted end of the cord round the shaft and wound the rest round his forefinger. As I leant forward to watch him, a twig snapped loudly against my arm. I held my breath, but no one noticed. All the attention now was on Windy. The rest of the band sat bravely on the fence.

"Not bloomin' well interested," said Squid quietly.

Windy drew back his arm and flung the dart. It passed over the bull's back and speared into the hedge just over my head.

"I'll get it for yer," offered Fat.

"No," ordered Squid. "Better wait till he's thrown anothery."

Windy was becoming braver every moment. He had faced the bull on foot; he had flung a dart; there was nothing to it.

"Git ready with y' lance there, Squid—I'll stir the old coot up. Watch this now."

He went at it like a javelin-thrower. The dart flashed from his hand. All at once the whole scene changed. Instead of a peaceful bull there was a bellowing monster with a dart in its neck charging the first thing it could see. The first thing was Windy. With the greatest ease Windy jumped the five-foot fence, darts still in hand. The bull's charge took it straight into the rails, which broke off rottenly. For a second I saw four fighters in mid-air, their faces horrified, and the bull head down after the horse. The horse shuddered all over and came to life with a bound, galloping away from underneath Squid. Squid sat in mid-air too, in a kind of horrified immobility. I had the illusion—at least I suppose it was an illusion—that while he sat there the bull passed under him, roaring horribly. The horse was headed for the bush, with the bull about fifty feet behind it.

Then the whole tableau resumed normal movement: boys landed on the earth, voices yelled, fragments of fence fell.

I knew I must clear out. Squid had enough friends to look after him. I crawled out and began running, keeping the hedge between me and the bullfighters. I ran towards Charlie Rolls' place, scrambled through a fence and looked about me.

The horse and bull were crashing in the bush. Well behind me I could hear banderilleros and the picador shouting faintly.

I was skirting Rolls' place when I saw, a long way ahead, the galloping horse. The bull was nowhere in sight. I was beginning to relax when I heard a fearful bellowing and saw Charlie Rolls' tent lift off the ground and plunge forward with a crashing of bottles and snapping of ropes. It lurched about the yard in a weird dance. Mrs Rolls appeared instantly at her back door, her face savage. One look at the dancing tent sent her scurrying inside. The tent collapsed in the vegetable patch, but picked itself up and went scudding over Charlie's "lawn" and collided with the front fence. This was too much for it. It rolled over a couple of times with further sounds of breaking bottles, then collapsed again with a baffled roar. The bull was wrapped up like a parcel.

Half the men and boys in the town were approaching the spot inside three minutes. There were shouts of "What is it?" and "Keep the women back," but no one went near it.

Mrs Rolls appeared with a pot-stick in her hand, her expression furious. "Disgusting!" she cried. "Disgusting!

How can he do it?" She evidently had the idea that Charlie's DTs had materialized in the backyard.

Just then Charlie himself emerged from the outdoor lavatory, hatless and white, shaking to the tips of his moustache. Above the din he cried, "Never again! Before Gawd, never again—" His tremolo was drowned by a fresh outburst of bellowing which sent the crowd scattering back.

"It's Donnelly's bull!" shouted someone, sighting the legs. "Where's Bill Donnelly?"

"Bill Donnelly!" went the cry.

But attention switched to Mrs Rolls who had rushed at her husband with the pot-stick. "See what you've done now—disgraced me before the whole town!" She hit him across the shoulders, screaming, "Drunkard! Sot! Animal!"

"Easy, easy!" shouted someone. "It's not his fault. I saw the bull rush in the tent m'self."

On the ground there was another outburst of bellowing, then a ripping sound and the bull's head appeared through the tent, the whites of its eyes showing and its tongue lolling.

"Shoot it," shouted someone.

But at this juncture Sergeant Gouvane appeared, in his hand a coil of rope which he fastened quickly round the hind-legs, then the front legs.

He stood up. "Where did this animal come from?"

"It was in the pound this morning," said someone.

The bull was now emitting deep, drawn-out moans, its head resting on the grass. The dart, I saw, was gone from its neck, but a trickle of blood came from the puncture.

"How did it get out of the pound?"

"Please, sir—" At the sound of this voice I swung round. There was Squid squeezing through the onlookers. The other bullfighters were hovering on the edge of the crowd. When I looked at Squid's face I saw every freckle standing out in its whiteness. It struck me that his mind must be wandering. "Please, sir—"

"Well?"

"I—we seen it get out—"

"'We'? Who?"

"Me an' Windy an'—"

"Hold on a minute." Gouvane took out his notebook. "All right—from the beginning now."

Squid was so shaken that his voice sounded piping and jerky, but he kept his head manfully.

"We was out for a horse ride near the poun'. I was having my go when we heard a fearful beller." He hesitated, casting his eyes wildly about the crowd. "We looks round an' there she is, charging out through the fence." For a time he couldn't continue. The crowd was silent. The bull was lying motionless now, still emitting regular moaning sounds.

"Go on," said Gouvane.

"I seen she might rush Windy an' Fat so I swung round me horse an' tried t' head her orf . . . ." He hesitated, looking abashed. "I'm not much of a rider an' I hadn't no saddle—I got pitched off."

"Then?"

"The bull chased the horse—an' that's about all . . . ."

His voice trailed away to nothing. He looked close to collapse. There was a murmur of admiration from the crowd.

"Did you see what frightened the bull in the first place?" demanded Gouvane.

Squid shook his head. "We couldn't see that part; we only heard her bellerin' suddenly."

"How is it," persisted Gouvane, "that for no apparent reason the bull—"

"Easy on him, sergeant," exclaimed someone. "The kid's pretty shocked. He's done damn' well if you ask me."

"I'm not asking you," said Gouvane coldly.

The crowd muttered a protest. At first Gouvane ignored them, but after a further question or two he relented.

That was all there was to it. On Monday the *Kananook Courier* came out with:

LOCAL BOY'S COURAGEOUS ACTION: FACES CHARGING
BULL TO DEFEND MATES.

Australia need not fear that the lofty spirit of Anzac is dead! The tradition of mateship was seen at its best when, on Saturday last, Birdwood Monash Peters, only son of Mrs A. M. Peters and the late Corporal Barney Peters, A.I.F., confronted a maddened bull belonging to Mr Thos Donnelly of Baxter Road and strove to turn it aside from its attack upon the persons of Joseph Gale, Michael Benson, Walter Wray and Ernest Ellison, his mates. The bull, which had been found wandering after breaking through a gate on Mr Donnelly's property, had been impounded that same morning by the Shire Ranger. The pound, as "The Courier" has repeatedly averred, is far from securely fenced. Indeed it is a matter of some wonder that the fence has not been forced ere this. It appears probable that for reasons unknown the bull took fright and plunged into the fence which thereupon broke. There is evidence that a sizeable sliver penetrated the neck of the beast. Maddened by pain and fear it charged the group of boys who happened to be exercising a horse there. Birdwood—living up to the reputation of his predecessor of glorious Gallipoli memory—interposed his horse between the enemy and his comrades . . . .

So it went on. At school old Moloney was sickening. After we had saluted the flag and said we loved God and our country, he called Squid up beside him on the school steps and read the *Courier* clipping aloud. Squid looked modestly at the ground.

"Three cheers for Birdie Peters. Hip, hip—"

The cheers stuck in my throat.

Afterwards I said to Squid, "How was the bull-fight?"

Without looking at me he said, "We didn't try it."

"That was a good shot of Windy Gale's," I said sourly.

He looked puzzled. "Don't know what you're talking about."

"Pity the fence broke," I persisted.

His expression didn't alter. He shrugged in a forgiving way. "If you make somethink up, who'll believe you?"

I knew the answer to that—no one.

But then he took a precaution. "Got an extra ticket for the flicks Sat'd'y," he said carelessly. "Reckon you might come?"

"No," I said. "No—I've seen enough bullfighting for a while."

"Okay," he said wearily. "Okay."

CHAPTER TWENTY-THREE

Squid's bullfight led indirectly to a number of happenings.

My father said, "I hope you congratulated Birdie on his courage."

When I didn't answer he looked over the top of the *Courier*: "Well, did you?"

"No," I admitted.

My mother said, "For such a nervous lad Birdie is to be admired."

"You said nothing?" my father persisted.

"I asked him how the bullfight went—"

"That was a grudging remark."

My mother said, "You'll have to be nice to him tonight, even if you do feel ungracious."

"Tonight?"

"We're invited over to Mrs Peters'."

I complained bitterly and tried to begin my version of Saturday's happenings.

"That's quite enough!" exclaimed my father. "I wish you would cultivate young Peters' friendship instead of fighting larrikins and riding camels."

I knew well enough that it was useless to argue. When my father left the room I said, "Why do we have to go to Peters'?"

"It happens to be our sixteenth wedding anniversary," said my mother coldly. "This afternoon when I was congratulating Mrs Peters she invited us in for a cup of tea and a few songs round the piano. For my part, I think it very nice of her."

It was a dreary evening. My father sang "Oh, Promise Me" to my mother and my mother sang "Because" to my father, and they sang "Until" together, while Mrs Peters trilled away at the piano.

The only alternative to listening to them was to escape with Squid to the Den. Although the singing sounded better from there, the Den was a dismal place at night and Squid's company didn't improve it. I could see he wanted to be pleasant to me. He probably reasoned that if he wasn't pleasant, I might still convince someone with my version of the bull incident. He kept telling me about coming attractions at the Palais and how he and I could see the next Tom Mix film, but every few sentences I interrupted him, calling him "the mighty picador" and "Big Chief Sitting Bull" and "Moloney's pet". This last really troubled him. There was something about Moloney beginning to worry him, but I couldn't see what it was at that stage.

When the singing ended we were called up for tea and cakes. My mother and father stood hand in hand as if they were about eighteen. "A night round the piano is really lovely," my mother was saying. "Young people nowadays only want to sit with the headphones on listening to the wrestling."

"Remember the operas when we were young?" my father put in. "Melba, John McCormack."

Mrs Peters, pouring the tea, said, "But Mr Reeve, some of the latest graphaphone records are good. Melba and Caruso, now, singing 'Les Miserables' from—from—"

"From *Lucia di Lammermoor*. That *was* singing. But gramophones are too expensive—"

"Funny you should say that, Mr Reeve. Only this morning I heard of a graphaphone likely to go cheap—a His Master's Voice belonging to Nettie McQueen. Poor soul; their place is getting auctioned."

A fateful remark this proved to be.

This was about all there was to the evening at the Peters'; but the news of the gramophone must have lodged in my mother's mind, because next morning she said to me, "Do you think you could bid at an auction sale?"

I supposed I could, though I had only a vague idea of how it was done. Nothing else was said for a day or two, except that I heard my father remark that they might be able to go to a pound for the gramophone if he went without a new hat.

McQueens' auction was not of much consequence in itself, but it set off a chain of other happenings involving both Johnno and myself. Johnno came with me to the auction and it was Johnno who was more concerned in the outcome than I was. I suppose we would never even have heard of the gramophone but for Mrs Peters, and certainly we would never have gone to Mrs Peters' but for my mother calling to congratulate her on Squid's courage. At the other end of the story, it was Johnno's composition called "The Auction" that caused his final clash with old Moloney and his father. I suppose if Squid hadn't gone bullfighting, then Johnno would never have made the final break.

We walked to the McQueens'. It was four miles by road, but by going through the bush behind the school almost a mile could be cut off. It was a hottish day and very clear, with the bush scents rising about us. As we would have to carry the gramophone if we got it, we were not expected home until fairly late. As a return for his help, Johnno had been invited to our place for tea.

Miss Beckenstall had made great changes in Johnno. She often passed books on to him, or asked him to write "brief descriptions" which she would discuss with him.

He read books and parts of books I had hardly heard of. Although she was equally encouraging to me, she was pushing Johnno ahead because he was older; probably, too, because she wanted to convince his father of his worth.

We walked south-east, with Lone Pine a mile off to the left, dark there and alone. In my mind it stood for something, but for what, I could scarcely have said.

"I suppose," said Johnno, "that after the sale they'll go away somewhere."

"Who?"

"The McQueens," he said.

I hadn't thought of this; I had only thought of the gramophone. I knew "Shadder" McQueen at school, but he seldom had much to do with me. The reason might have been that my mother sometimes passed my clothes on to him. These clothes were pretty much worn by me and by a city cousin who wore them first.

Mr McQueen had an orchard, but according to my father it was losing money. McQueen also had a rabbit round, in fact, meals at the McQueens' were said to be mostly rabbit and fruit. This was in all probability true, as Shadder usually took fruit or rabbit-legs to school for lunch. He would trade these sometimes for a sandwich or a piece of cake, but the offer generally had to come from someone else.

Mr McQueen had been gassed at the war and two or three times had collapsed in his cart during his rabbit round, leaving the horse to take him home. When my mother heard about this she bought rabbits every week till even Gyp was sick of them.

As if he were continuing my thoughts Johnno said, "My old man says they owe money to the council and to Harrison's store and a hell of a lot of money to the bank."

"It must be pretty bad," I said absently.

We were climbing the last hill, coming out of the heath country into apple orchards which stretched away to Western Port. We could see McQueen's house on the ridge, a small, single-gabled place. As we came nearer we noticed a red SALE flag by the front window.

CHAPTER TWENTY-FOUR

The number on the gramophone was 124. By the time it was put up for auction late afternoon had come and I was beginning to feel as unhappy as Johnno. I had noticed Shadder watching from a distance, or helping his mother prepare cups of tea. The sight of him made me feel guilty. Inside, the house was practically empty. People tramped through it looking about the walls for damp, examining the bathroom, seeing that the doors opened properly. They left mud on the floors and talked loudly about the worn bath-heater and the worn linoleum and the leak in the back veranda roof. Johnno kept scowling all the time, and when the gramophone was put up he moved away from me.

"What's next, Harold?"

Mr Bolter the auctioneer was a man with an enormous voice. He could begin quietly, almost in a whisper, then gradually build up to a shout. He could close his eyes to slits or open them like searchlights. Standing there on the back of a spring-cart, with his thumb in his waistcoat arm-hole and his face red from shouting, he was watching the crowd shrewdly.

"Number one two four, one His Master's Voice graphaphone and assortment of recuds," answered Harold. He held it over his head. It was a table model, dark red and shining. "Good as noo, Mr Bolter."

"You're right, Harold, you're right; good as new. Lift it up here and let the ladies and gents hear a record. What've we got now?"

Harold held a record at arm's length. "Jesu Joy of Man's Desirin'—"

"Something bright, Harold, eh? Religion's all right in its place—"

"'When I Was Twenty-One', sung by Harry Lauder."

"That's the stuff!"

Harry Lauder's voice rose thinly over the crowd:

> "Oh, when I was twenty-one,
> When I was twenty-one,
> I never ha' lots o' monie,
> But I'd always lots o' fun—"

"All right, Harold, shut it off now. What am I offered, ladies and gents? I should ask a tenner for this beautiful talking machine fashioned by the master-craftsmen of HMV; but I'll make it only a fiver—"

My heart sank. Johnno caught my eye from several paces away. "We won't be guilty of taking it, anyway," said his glance.

"A fiver. Who'll offer me a fiver for this good-as-new HMV table gramophone—twelve-inch plush-covered turntable, gooseneck tone arm; the latest thing in gramophones and a dozen records thrown in."

No one spoke. Mr Bolter looked astonished. "Four poun' ten?"

Some of the men began to drift away. Most of them were after furniture, or implements; a gramophone was a luxury.

"Four quid am I bid? Just four quid to start off this glorious instrument?"

Most of the men weren't even looking his way. He lowered the hammer slowly. "Ladies and gents, I beg you now, be serious; think what you'd be getting—an HMV luxury-model gramophone." No one spoke. "Where's your culture, ladies and gents?" he asked despairingly.

In the doorway behind him I saw Mrs McQueen and Shadder, Mrs McQueen holding her apron between her hands. Mr Bolter leant forward and with eyes nearly closed said, "Am I bid five bob, then? A dollar for this—"

"Yes," I said.

"Well!" He put his hands on his hips and looked at me. "Five bob from young Charlie Reeve here; five bob from a boy who knows his culture. Five bob I'm bid. Any advance on five bob? Five bob for the cultural mechanism in highly finished cedar. Who'll offer me seven and six?"

He was speaking rapidly, his left arm raised, his cheeks quivering. "Five bob it is, five bob . . . . Seven and six—thank you, madam." I glanced to where he was looking but no woman was there. "Seven and six, seven and six for the musical glories of Beethoven and Mo-zart, seven and six is all I'm asking—"

"Ten shillings," I said.

"Young Reeve again and the offer is ten bob; just a half-note for this technically perfect de luxe model gramophone, ten bob from young Reeve—"

Beyond him I saw Mrs McQueen again and Shadder, both watching closely. It must have seemed impossible that their one luxury was to go for ten shillings. I glanced towards Johnno. He was kicking the turf with his toe, looking down at the ground unhappily.

"A pound," I said.

Mr Bolter stopped short and drew a breath. "Now just a minute, young feller! Yours was the ten bob bid. You understand that?"

"Yes," I said.

I heard some laughs from the crowd.

192

"You *want* to make it a pound?"

"Yes," I repeated self-consciously.

He drew himself up. "Have you *got* a pound?"

I went to take it from my pocket, forgetting it was pinned there with a safety pin. The crowd laughed while I undid the pin and held the note up.

"A quid it is, by God. Very well, I'll make it a pound. Here's a boy who really appreciates the glories of Melba and Crusoe. One pound, ladies and gentlemen, any advance—"

"Twenty-five bob," said Johnno, coming over to me.

"What!" I exclaimed.

Mr Bolter was about to race on, but he hesitated. Johnno said to me, "I bid for you."

"I've only got a pound."

"Here." He thrust five shillings into my hand.

"Just what goes on here, lads? No funny business, now. We've hardly got an hour left before dark and a lot to do. What's it to be now and who's it from?"

"Twenty-five bob," hissed Johnno, jabbing me with his arm.

"Twenty-five," I repeated aloud.

"Twenty-five bob it is," declared Mr Bolter, narrowing his eyes. "Twenty-five bob and don't say I didn't warn you. Twenty-five bob and it's going, twenty-five bob, any advance on twenty-five bob? Going at twenty-five bob. Going, going—" He crashed the hammer down, then pointed the handle towards me. "Twenty-five bob to

193

get from young Reeve there, Harold. What his father will say next time I'm up at the council chambers I don't know."

I handed Harold the twenty-five shillings and bewilderedly took the gramophone on my hip. Johnno picked up the records.

"And now, ladies and gents, the poultry and contents of one shed situate at rear of residence."

The crowd moved away, leaving Johnno and me standing there. A few people grinned amusedly as they passed. When they had gone I said, "What did you do that for?"

"Same reason as you called a pound," he said.

"But I don't know when we can pay you back."

"It doesn't matter," he said. "I got it for overtime from Mr Hayes."

We stood about undecidedly. The auctioneer's voice was continuing at the back of the house. Nearer at hand a few men were loading furniture on a lorry. The sun was shining horizontally on the front of the house and the surrounding apple-blossom. Mrs McQueen and Shadder had gone inside.

"Do we have to wait?" asked Johnno.

"No," I said, "Let's go."

The main result of the auction as far as Johnno and I were concerned was still over a month away. In the meantime the gramophone became something of a novelty. For weeks after the sale we had boys dropping in after school to listen to records.

One result of this was that Squid became envious. Late one afternoon while I was out he asked if he could play a few records on his own. Next day "Gundagai" stuck on ". . . once more". Peter Dawson would come up to the words at full gallop,

> *"And the pals of my childhood*
> *Once more—"*

"Once more," he'd say again, "once more, once more, once more—"

"He dug it with a pocket knife!" claimed Ian accusingly.

"Nonsense!" cried my mother.

It was no good; Squid could do no wrong at our place.

CHAPTER TWENTY-FIVE

It was now the beginning of November. At the end of the month we were to sit for the Merit. The prospect hung over all we did and was hardly out of our conversation. Every time old Moloney passed me he glanced at me as if I had already failed. Only Miss Beckenstall was encouraging. "Concentrate and you'll do it," she said. "Refuse to be diverted for a moment."

My father kept me studying each night—geography, geometry, grammar . . . . Most of the evenings ended the same way: "Good God, boy, why don't you pay attention? How do you expect to get a job if you dream? I tell you, we're coming into the hardest times we've known. If you don't apply yourself . . . ." And so on.

I was sleeping on the veranda again now. After these homework sessions it was always a relief to go out there and hear the sea washing on the beach and see the red light flashing at the end of the pier. Life as pictured by adults was hell.

On Saturday afternoons there was some let-up. Johnno and I were allowed then to take Grandfather McDonald's boat about a mile out to the reef, mainly because we often caught flathead there. The boatshed reminded me always of Grandfather's death and of Gyp barking in the fog. It was deserted and lonely, the sea sounding in it as if in a shell. It smelt of oil and salt and dried bait. The boat's motor had not been run for months, as petrol was always considered a luxury, so wherever we went we rowed. As the exams drew nearer we took books out with us, but except for things we really enjoyed—the death of Burke and Wills, the spearing of Kennedy and so on—we did little. Gyp usually came with us, taking up a position in the bows like a figurehead.

Usually we came back from the reef late in the afternoon and anchored over the wreck of the *Isis*. She was down about twelve feet, dark-looking and dead. Johnno would pull himself down to her on the anchor chain, his body gleaming under the water like a great white fish. Sometimes I followed him uneasily. With singing ears we moved along the hull, holding to whatever offered, shut in by green walls of sea. Sand had already covered part of the bows, and whitebait darted in shoals from the cabin. Seaweed waved back and forth even when there was scarcely a wave above us. It was hard to believe as we shot into sunlight that the underwater world existed. We would hold on at the stern, dazzled by the sun, the water perfectly calm all round us.

It was during these days before the Merit that Armistice Day came. Squid was generally the star of the occasion, but this year there was another star. I was late for the special assembly and didn't hear the guest announced; in fact, I had to join our line by dodging behind trees. He was a tall, gangling man with a thatch of grey hair but a boyish face.

"I want to say," he said, "how proud I am to be in the land of those who so bravely and determinedly supported us in the world war of 1917–18."

But there was something peculiar about his voice. He had actually said, "Ah wanna say . . . ."

Fat Benson leant over and whispered, "He's American."

A shock of disappointment hit me. All through the two minutes' silence my mental pictures of the war were upset by the thought that probably even Tom Mix spoke this same way.

As "one bereaved by the war" and "one who had recently shown he was by no means lacking the courage of his father", Squid was able to meet the American. At lunch-time he told us in a twanging voice that the visitor was installing "the biggest Wurlitzer organ in the Southern Hemisphere" at some picture theatre in the city. "Sure sounds a mighty instrument," he added.

Squid was riding high these days. Only Miss Beckenstall doubted him. She might well have doubted him—as I happened to find out.

A couple of days before the exams, I left my geography book at school. When my father came home he said, "Back you go and get it before you sit down for tea."

When I got there the cleaners were working at the infants' end of the school; the rest of the place was deserted. Outside, every blade of grass and every post and step and wall and tree-trunk was tired and kicked-looking. Our room still held the odours and worries of the past day. I was walking up the sloping floor to the back when I heard a voice above me say, "G'day."

I swung round. Standing near the top of a long ladder was Squid, looking down like some sort of bird. The ladder was leaning against the wall over the blackboard, beside the picture of Sappho.

"Getting me pen," he explained.

It had been stuck in the ceiling for weeks, not far above Sappho's head.

"Thought you'd bought another."

"Did too, but in the exam a feller might need an extra one." He reached up and pulled it out. "Reckon you might give us a lift with the ladder?"

We carried it out and put it back behind the shelter-shed. There was something queer about Squid as we walked back; something more than usually secretive.

"I've got to get my geography book," I said. "I'll catch up."

He didn't answer, but walked slowly towards the gate, studying his pen concernedly.

Back in the empty room I picked up my book. Passing Squid's desk I stopped and looked again at Sappho. In the dust on her glass something was written. I moved my head this way and that till I saw clearly: Area O π R2; Circum. O π D. I sat in Squid's desk. It was all clear from there:

$$\text{Int.} = \frac{\text{PRT};}{100} \text{ annulus } \pi(R + r)(R - r),$$

$$\text{area } \Delta \frac{\text{vert. ht.} \times b}{2}$$

—line after line of it.

Squid was away next day. Mrs Peters said it was his old stomach trouble. "Been working so hard at algebra and all that . . . ."

He thought things out well, did Squid, as became apparent later. It was no good just having a plan; you also had to have a second plan in case the first failed. In the meantime I had never seen him more confident.

The fearful day came. We knew then the atmosphere of a jail when a man is about to be hanged. There was bravado from a few of the boys, but Johnno and I hardly spoke and Squid kept to himself. He'd got out of bed for the exam and really shouldn't have come. His breakfast was repeating on him and he had spots in front of his eyes.

We had been having windy, unsettled weather, but the day of the Merit was perfectly calm—as if to contrast with our feelings.

Sitting at my desk I looked at the picture of Sappho. From there I could read nothing. Squid was leaning back, looking vaguely around the walls. I realized he'd been doing this a lot lately, no doubt as part of his preparation.

Miss Beckenstall, with a sheaf of the dreaded arithmetic papers in her hand, was just saying good morning when Moloney came in and whispered something to her, his cropped nicotined moustache against her ear.

"Now?"

"At once," he said.

"Boys and girls, we are to change rooms with grade six, as Mr Moloney wishes to write their geography examination on their blackboard."

I looked at Squid. His mouth had fallen open and his face had turned to wax.

Moloney took over. "Bring pens, pencils and rulers only."

There was the sound of these items being gathered up. Squid was motionless, staring into space.

"Birdwood Peters," said Miss Beckenstall sharply.

He came to himself and gathered his belongings. He stared a moment at Sappho, perhaps trying to memorize every formula on her face.

"Class, stand," commanded Moloney. "Row one—to the other room, quick march. Row two, follow on."

We were going through the other door when I saw Squid clutch his stomach with his free hand. He spun on his feet like a shot Indian and collapsed on the floor. There were shrieks from the girls and envious looks from the boys.

"Give him air!" shouted Moloney. "Everyone sit down. Miss Beckenstall—water."

While all this was going on Squid was moaning quietly, his mouth open, his freckles clear on his pale face.

"He's dying," whispered Mary Hogan. "He's dying, he's dying; I know he's—"

"Ah, shut up!" hissed Stinger from behind her. "It's only his gut."

Miss Beckenstall returned with water. Moloney, who was supporting Squid's head, held out his hand for the cup. Somehow their two hands collided and Squid got the lot in the face. He jerked to life, but had the presence of mind to sink back again, muttering feebly. Miss Beckenstall smiled grimly.

Old Moloney carried him outside. After, so we heard, he was taken home lying on the seat of one of Jonas's cabs, Moloney going with him. While we did our first examination, Miss Beckenstall copied Moloney's geography questions on the blackboard for grade six.

Squid was back a couple of days later. By then he was fit to do the exam, even though he was still suffering from heartburn and dizzy spells. He did it alone in our room. By that time, with Johnno's help to bunk me up, I had run a broom over Sappho's face. I daresay Squid had managed to find out all about the paper by then, though, for he passed; in fact he passed everything.

To the surprise of everyone but Miss Beckenstall Johnno and I both got through our Merit. Our respective fathers gave us sixpence to go downstairs at the pictures, and altogether life at home changed for both of us. But this was only the calm before the storm.

At the end of the year, when everything was becoming relaxed and there was a holiday feeling in the air, Miss Beckenstall set us a composition subject: "An Occasion I Shall Always Remember". I daresay she gave it only to fill in time. We finished it before lunch, then Johnno and I went off to climb Lone Pine.

The old tree already seemed like something belonging to the past. We were, after all, almost third form high-school students, and climbing trees was slightly beneath us. But in some way the tree meant a good deal to us. For years it had been a place of escape, and perhaps we knew even then that we would always associate it with our periods of freedom.

Sitting on the board at the top Johnno said to me from the other side of the trunk, "I called my composition, 'The Auction'."

"About McQueens'?"

"Sort of. I didn't give any name, though."

We could see the McQueens' house from the tree, far off to the south-east, a small white shape.

I said, "What did you say about it?"

I couldn't see his face, only his hand holding the trunk.

"I wrote just the way it hit me: you know, the blossom and the people gathered round and Mrs McQueen looking sad—all that sort of thing. Miss Beckenstall has been saying to let myself go about something, so that's what I did."

It turned out to be a disastrous composition.

Miss Beckenstall, who was soon to get married, was away that afternoon and old Moloney decided to correct the composition himself. While we filled in time working out problems, he sat at the table making red ink comments on each page. Every now and then he'd say something like "Good work, Birdie" or "How do you spell 'divine', Janet Baker?" or "Try to, Wray, 'try to'. 'Try and' is a contradiction in terms."

204

When he came to Johnno's he said after a bit, "What might this be, Johnston?" He made several jabs at it with his pen.

I glanced back at Johnno. He flushed slightly, but went on with his work.

"Do you hear me, Johnston?"

"It was a sort of experiment, sir," said Johnno slowly.

Moloney made a snorting sound. "Really, your attempts to portray this house and these people are peculiar, to say the least. Whoever heard of a 'blossomed tree' or—"

"No sir," said Johnno faintly.

"What d' you mean 'no sir'?"

"I—don't know," admitted Johnno.

"Well, think before you speak," replied Moloney, "and before you write, too." He went on correcting for some time, his grunts and jabs becoming more frequent. Finally he stood up holding Johnno's composition in his hands. "I believe I should read this—this—extraordinary effusion."

He was standing beside my desk with it.

"No sir," gasped Johnno.

"I beg your pardon?"

Johnno simply shook his head while everyone looked at him.

"You add insolence to incompetence, Johnston."

In a ridiculing voice, Moloney began reading aloud: "'I can see it still: the auctioneer on the spring-cart shouting to the crowd, all the private things: the beds and saucepans and chairs and mirrors on the grass. The crowd laughing. The two alone at the door'—no verbs, you'll observe. Our friend Johnston needs no verbs, or sense either. 'It seemed wrong then that the sun was shining on the blossomed trees . . . .'"

I glanced back at Johnno. His face was white. There were titters from the girls and even a few laughs from the boys, but Johnno's friends looked down at their desks saying nothing.

Moloney read then about the woman holding her apron between her hands.

Johnno rose slowly to his feet, staring at the book in Moloney's hands.

Moloney read on remorselessly.

"Please sir—"

Either Moloney didn't hear him or he ignored him.

All at once Johnno leant down and plucked out his inkwell and flung it. It hit Moloney's chest with such force that he doubled up, jerking his glasses to the floor. At first there wasn't a sound. There stood Johnno, white as a sheet, and Moloney blinking beside me and holding his chest, the ink soaking into his shirt front, the composition still in his hand.

"Stamp on his glasses," hissed Stinger.

I reached out my foot and heard the glass crunch under my heel.

"I—I'm sorry, sir," I heard Johnno say.

Moloney raised his head slowly. In a hoarse voice he said, "Out! Out with you both. The police will hear about this, I assure you. Your parents, Reeve, will pay for my spectacles—every penny. Get out."

He hadn't moved from his position. The class was speechless, everyone staring unbelievingly as if the ink had been blood. Johnno remained in his place, his mouth half open. My heart was booming in my ears.

"Out!"

We clattered from the classroom together, out down the steps and into the empty grounds. Without a word we walked across the cricket pitch and climbed the fence and entered the bush. Somewhere among the trees we stopped and looked at each other. "I didn't know anyone but Miss Beckenstall would read it," said Johnno in a strained voice.

I couldn't answer. In my ears was the crunching of Moloney's glasses, a sound I can hear yet. To think of it and of the next twenty-four hours is to be a boy again.

"He'll go to my old man," said Johnno flatly. "Anyhow, I'm done for." He looked at me hopelessly. "What do we do?"

I had no idea. We tried to talk about it; perhaps, after all, Moloney would say nothing. All we could do was go home and if we heard him coming, we could clear out.

"Where?" I said.

"Anywhere," answered Johnno. "Otways, Queensland —anywhere."

CHAPTER TWENTY-SIX

So we went home. Nothing happened at our place, but I could hardly speak a word all through tea.

"What's the matter with you?" asked my father.

"I feel sick," I said—which was true.

"You'd better get to bed early, then."

As soon as it was dark I went out on the veranda and lay down without undressing. It was moonlight and very still, and for late November cool and misty. The light winked at the end of the pier and the answering lights far out in the channel winked back. Everything was the same—lights, stars, house, sea; everything except me. I listened for Moloney coming, but there was no sound of him. I could hear voices faintly from the pier and the sea lapping and then the squealing of Peters' new loudspeaker, and a voice saying "3LO Melbourne, the time is now eight-thirty . . . ."

I must have been lying there half an hour when a pebble landed on the veranda. I sat up and saw someone moving in the tea-tree beside the house. Dropping over the edge of the veranda, I went into the shadow.

A girl's voice whispered, "Charlie!"

Peering, I saw Eileen, the moonlight blanching her face.

"What's happened?"

"Fred's gone," she said.

Eileen, who was always sure of herself, began crying. I took hold of her arm and led her away from the house.

"Mr Moloney came and told us," she said. "Dad lost his temper and hit Fred in front of him." The words came tumbling out so quickly that I could hardly follow what she was saying.

"If only he hadn't hit back. He only hit once, but when he did dad punched him terribly and he didn't try to protect himself."

I felt sick. "Where is he?"

She shook her head. "I followed him to the Island, but lost him."

We stood there, not knowing what to do. The Island was a strip of coast between the beach and the creek, only wide enough for a road and a row of houses. Except at holiday time, the houses were empty, their doors locked and their blinds drawn. I remembered that Johnno had said once that if a chap was stuck, if he was turned out of his home, he could find shelter there.

"I might be able to find him," I said.

"I brought food for him," said Eileen. "He's had nothing."

In the shadows, picking up the parcel, we heard a horse and jinker on the gravel road. It pulled up at our gate and old Moloney got out. He was bare-headed, his scalp shining in the moonlight. When he had gone to our front door, out of our sight, I said, "We can go down the cliffs to the beach."

"I'll go home," said Eileen. "It will make things worse if I stay."

She handed me the food, but I was hardly noticing her. My mind was on Moloney and my father.

"It's upset him terribly."

"Upset—?"

"Dad—he's been sitting with his head in his hands ever since—"

"I must go," I said.

I left her there and ran towards the path down the cliffs. Just then I heard the veranda door open, and my father striding round to my bed.

"Charlie!" And as he got nearer, "Why didn't you tell us about this?"

I hesitated at the top of the path. "Charlie," I heard more loudly, "you had better come in at once."

I almost turned back. Inside, through the open door, I could see the light shining on Moloney's head and my mother holding Ian by the hand.

"Charlie!"

I went softly down the path. Before me the moon shone on the sea, silhouetting tea-tree to either side. I would go, I thought, to the spot where Eileen had last seen him, and would look for him at each house.

I came on to the beach and began following it north-east, walking at the water's edge. The tide was nearly full, but there was not so much as a ripple on the sea. I crossed the bridge at the mouth of the creek and went on along the Island.

All this part of the Island was flat except for low dunes behind the beach. Tea-tree grew thickly on these dunes, all bent inland and matted together. I stopped and looked about uneasily. Ahead lay the calm sea and white beach stretching as clear as day and the tea-tree black and somehow sad-looking. The tea-tree stood between the sea and the week-end houses, its tops growing so densely together that in places you could lie on them, and if it were windy you could feel the spindly trunks swaying beneath. Underneath this roof of leaves the sound of the sea was deadened even on the roughest days. Instead, you heard only the creaking of trunks as if the trees were whispering. Tracks came over the dunes from the beach and led to the houses—to "Warrawee" and "This'll Do" and "Wy Wurrie". They were flimsy houses most of them, their roofs rusting, their paint all faded. Except in holiday time, they were silent.

I went into the tea-tree uneasily. The moon shone on the tracks, but under the trees was black. I went to the fence-line of the houses and looked at them hunched under their trees, the branches touching their sides. There was no light anywhere.

I stopped outside the first house and called Johnno's name. My voice sounded so loud that I moved back into the shadows. It would be better to go right up to the walls, I thought, and call softly.

I dragged open the gate of "Trawalla" and went up a sandy path to the veranda. As I stepped onto it the boards creaked, starting a bumping of rabbits underneath. I dodged a Coolgardie safe and a stack of banksia logs and a quoit-peg.

"Johnno!"

I listened but could hear nothing. He would go farther, I thought; this was too close to the town. But I continued to go into each house, calling and listening.

At "Warrawee" there was a window with undrawn blinds. I rubbed away the salt and looked inside. The moon shone on empty vases and shells and last year's Christmas decorations. I tried to see into the shadow, but might as well have been blind.

"Johnno!"

I heard only my own heart. It had been booming ever since we had left the school. A cat came miaowing out of the shadows, stiff-tailed and friendly. For a while I hung on to it, listening to it purring, wishing the whole thing had never happened.

I said more loudly, "Johnno!"

The cat struggled down and ran into the darkness. I returned to the track in front of the houses. Everywhere smelt of salt and rust and of the dusty bark of the tea-tree. I stopped and peered into "This'll Do" wondering whether it was worth going in. As I looked I heard a voice behind me.

I swung about. Johnno stood very still, the moon shining on his face, his face all bruised and cut, his lips so swollen that they changed his voice. I found I couldn't speak.

He said softly, "I'm clearing out."

When I didn't say anything, he said, "I hit my dad."

"Yes," I said.

"Eileen told you?"

"Yes."

He kicked at the sand, glancing down at his feet. "She was mad, too?"

"No, just worried. She gave me some food for you."

He shook his head. "I don't feel hungry." He stood thinking for a bit, then he said, "Could you, do you think, do something for me?"

"Anything you like," I said.

"Could you—" he began slowly, "could you, d' you reckon, row me across the bay?"

I breathed deeply. "To Queenscliff?"

"Yes," he said.

Now that the time had come the idea frightened me. But what was I to do myself? Johnno was waiting for me to answer.

"All right," I said. "I'll go with you."

"We'd better start, then," said Johnno.

CHAPTER TWENTY-SEVEN

We kept to the tea-tree till we came to the place where the creek turned sharply to its outlet through the sand. At the bridge we watched awhile, but no one was near it. The mouth of the creek was boarded to stop drifting sand and in this part of it, fishing boats lay motionless. We crossed over and walked quickly towards the pier. Along that part of the beach the Olivers were hauling in their nets, stepping towards each other along the beach. We could see the moving water where the fish were trapped and hear the men's low voices. Under the pier we stopped and looked towards our boatshed and up the cliffs to the house. Every light was on, but about the beach there was no one. I felt lonely suddenly, wishing I were back on the veranda, Moloney or no Moloney.

We went separately to the base of the cliff and lay flat there, listening and watching. There was only a lapping from the sea and someone laughing a long way off. I felt surprised that anyone could laugh so happily when we felt the way we did. We edged round the base of the cliff towards the boatshed and hid in the tea-tree. There was no sound from the house, but presently we heard Peters' wireless squeal a few times and a voice say, "We are now taking you over to community singing at the Prahran town hall."

"Can we get the door open?"

"I think so," I said. "I'll go and try."

I crept behind the shed, then along the shadowy side of it. Sand had drifted half-way up the wall, so it was almost possible to step on the roof. I hid in the shadows there, listening. It was hard to hear anything for the noise of community singing, but after a few minutes the wireless was switched off.

I went slowly to the door and drew the latch. If my father came I could say that Johnno and I had been for a walk and had thought of going for a row in the moonlight—which would be true, or partly true.

I lifted the sagging doors, and smelt the usual smell of bait and oil and salt. Inside lay the sleeping boat, the moonlight touching its bows. Johnno appeared at my side without a sound and we began hauling together. We did the noisy part quickly, pulling the boat with strong tugs out of the shed and on to the sand. We hid then, watching from the shadows. No one came. From the house we could hear nothing except the occasional slam of a door. We went back and hauled the boat quickly down to the water's edge, then I ran back for oars and rowlocks while Johnno began trampling our footmarks. Then he came backwards down the beach, scattering sand from a baling tin.

"Get in," he whispered. "I'll push her out."

We had begun to move when a sound struck us motionless—a single excited bark. Gyp came running on to the beach, making pleased, gurgling sounds in his throat.

"Hell," muttered Johnno, "what'll we do?"

I shook my head. "If we don't take him he'll howl."

"Let him in, then."

I clicked my fingers, and when he came I lifted him over the stern then got in myself. He took up his figure-head position, pointing his nose across the Bay. Johnno stripped off his clothes and pushed us till the water was up to his chest, then he scrambled in.

For a full minute we sat listening. No one up at the house moved. In Peters' all the lights had gone out, which meant it was half-past nine. Johnno wrapped his singlet round the blade of one oar and his underpants round the other and wet the leathers where they passed through the rowlocks. Then I began rowing, dipping the blades quietly, lying back hard. Phosphorus spun brightly in the water.

"Charlie!" The voice came from the veranda.

I stopped rowing. It was hard not to answer. Gyp looked round, sensing something was wrong.

"If you like," whispered Johnno, "you could give it away—"

He had put on his trousers and shirt and was sitting in the stern.

"No," I said. "No." The words came from me almost involuntarily.

I began rowing strongly, keeping Johnno's head lined up with our house lights.

"Charlie!" Already my father's voice was less distinct. I kept pulling hard. Slowly the house lights drew away. The water rippled alongside; behind us our wake glittered in the moonlight. They have only to look this way, I thought, and we're done.

"The tide's on the turn," said Johnno. I didn't answer.

The pier light fell behind. It blinked on my left, while the house lights were still directly behind. The air was cool, but already the rowing was warming me. I rowed hard, feeling the need to hurry away in case I weakened and decided against it all. Johnno sat in the stern bathing his face with his handkerchief. His eyes were black and swollen and the corner of his mouth was bleeding still.

The house lights and the pier light drew together and fell lower on the horizon. Johnno said, "If you like I'll row a bit."

"No," I said. "No, I'll keep going."

Now and then Gyp's tail swished against my back. He was making impatient sounds in his throat, as if anxious to get to wherever we were going.

"Let's have a go," said Johnno again.

I changed over with him, the boat moving slightly under us.

Johnno sat down. "If you keep me lined up with the channel light it should be about right," he said.

I sat in the stern with my head in my hands. It struck me that I was a fool to run away. After all, I could have worked somewhere to pay for Moloney's glasses and could have apologized and put up with a hiding. But then there was Johnno. It didn't surprise me that Johnno was determined not to go back. He had been thrashed at home and at school for as long as I had known him—and as far as I could see, he had seldom deserved it. Now he had hit back. It was the end as far as he was concerned.

I said, "Eileen told me that after you had gone he sat with his head in his hands wishing he had never done it."

"My dad?"

"Yes."

He sat with the oars raised, looking beyond me. He said presently, "He's belted me dozens of times."

"He's had plenty to worry about," I said, repeating remarks of my father's.

"I dare say," Johnno admitted. I thought he was reconsidering things, but he suddenly struck hard with the oars and I saw there was no hope of going back. I leant on my knees again. Since I'd stopped rowing it seemed much colder. I looked back over my shoulder. The house lights and even the pier lights had gone. I looked away, then looked back again, but sure enough they had gone. Beyond Johnno's head was the channel light flashing brightly. Westward I could see lights far off on the other side of the bay. A funny thing that, I thought: we were closer to the east side, but we could see nothing of it.

"Anyhow," said Johnno, "I'd never get to the high school now. Probably I'd have to keep working at Digger Hayes'."

"You passed your Merit, and Miss Beckenstall would always help."

"He'd never let me go after what happened."

"My father says he was always keen for you to have a good education."

"He always *said* he was keen, but he bashed me so much when I didn't know things that I couldn't think— that's true, Charlie, I couldn't think. It was the same with old Moloney. Only Miss Beckenstall was any good."

Johnno had paused again with the oars raised. He said all at once, "Why can't we see the pier lights?"

"They've dropped out of sight," I said. Then I realized this was a stupid remark.

"Some of the stars have gone too," said Johnno.

I turned round. The stars low in the sky were blotted out, but higher up they were bright. A slight breeze passed us, then dropped off, then came again, blowing off the land very gently. Johnno was still sitting with the oars raised.

"That's fog," he said. "It's a long way off."

He unwrapped the oars and began rowing hard while I waved him port or starboard, keeping him on the channel light. I looked back over my shoulder. I could see car lights coming down Chapman's Hill; down, down, then all at once they vanished.

"It's fog all right."

Johnno didn't answer. He was sending the boat skimming along easily. The sound of the rowlocks and of the swishing water were all we could hear. He said, between breaths, "So long as we can see the other side we're right."

I looked unhappily ahead. Gyp was still in the bows, ears flapping and nose raised, every hair of him clear in the moonlight. The sight of him kept reminding me of home. He expected, I supposed, to go for a row then come back and go to his bed under the house. A few hundred yards beyond him was the channel light and many miles beyond that the few lights of the other side.

"Pull left," I said. My voice sounded unreal.

"How far to the channel?"

"You're nearly there."

I glanced back over my shoulder. The fog didn't look any nearer. It was deeper perhaps, but still a long way off. It was pale grey in the moonlight and away above it were the stars. There was no sign of the town; it had gone completely.

The light on top of the piles was lighting the boat now with a reddish glare.

"That's three miles," said Johnno as we came up to it. "How long has it taken?"

"I don't know," I said. It seemed like hours. Neither of us had watches. "About an hour, I suppose."

"We could make the other side before sunrise."

"There's the fog," I said.

He stopped rowing again and we both looked at it.

"It's nearer, I think."

He agreed reluctantly. "But it might stop at that."

"I don't reckon."

We sat undecidedly for a moment.

"What's that sound?"

"It's a foghorn somewhere."

"Not that—a sound like a creek running."

He peered around us, listening carefully. "It's the tide—it's running between the piles under the light. I suppose it's starting to go out."

It was a faint, but somehow threatening sound.

"Maybe we should tie up to the piles till we see what the fog does."

"In the morning they'd find us," he said. "There we'd be, picked up in everyone's binoculars, then the motor-boats would come out."

This didn't seem such a terrible prospect.

"If we need to tie up," he went on, "we can make for one of the lights in the channel on the other side." He began rowing again.

"We'd better angle a bit to allow for the current," I suggested.

"Yes, I hadn't thought of it."

He swung the boat round a little while I lined him up on a light on the other side of the bay. Then he rowed solidly for, half a mile or more.

"I'll give you a rest."

He was breathing hard, but he shook his head. "Both of us had better row."

I went and sat next to him and we took an oar each. The red light astern had a misty look about it. We tried to keep it at an angle to the right, but gradually we swung round and had to correct ourselves. Then the light disappeared altogether.

"Maybe if you sit in the stern and guide me—"

"I'll have a go at the rowing," I said.

He went back reluctantly and put me on course, then bathed his face again. The blood still trickled from the corner of his mouth and his eyes were ghastly to look at.

To myself I said, "Forward, back. Forward, back," breathing rhythmically.

It was still bright moonlight and still the phosphorus glittered at the tips of the oars. Once or twice I forgot the fog and even forgot we were running away. The rhythm of the rowing and the aching of my arms and back stopped much thinking at all, but then Gyp licked my neck and woke me again to our situation.

The fog crept on us unawares. We could see the western lights and the stars above us, then in less than a minute, nothing; nothing at all. A white void closed in so that I even saw Johnno all shrouded in mist. His voice came to me dismally, "What do we do now?"

I rested on the oars. Overhead we could still see the moon. It had been at an angle to our left. If we kept it that way, I said, maybe we could keep going. When we had agreed, I began rowing again, but I had little faith that we'd reach the other side.

The fog deepened and the moon became less distinct. Far off still we could hear the foghorn. Gyp gave an impatient whimper.

"Shut up!" I said.

He pushed against me as if apologizing and I noticed that his fur was wet with mist.

"Sit!" I exclaimed between breaths. He sighed and curled himself behind me. In the stern Johnno was hunched miserably. Somehow the fog made his face look terrible—as if he were looking through a parted curtain at something that horrified him.

"It's no good," I said at last. "I can't see it."

Johnno lifted his head and looked above us, then let his glance fall dismally to the bottom of the boat. He said like a small boy, "I don't want to go back."

The foghorn answered him dolefully, still far off.

"We can't get anywhere," I said. "We've got nothing left to guide us."

The boat was rocking a little, very little.

"Give me a go," he said.

"You can if you like—but which way?"

It didn't seem to matter to him just then; mainly he needed something to do. He rowed for fifteen minutes or more, sometimes glancing hopelessly around him. Watching him I felt we could easily enough be going in circles. Now and then the mists thinned and once broke overhead. The moon was on our left, which meant we were rowing towards home. Johnno furrowed his brow. "Hell, I'm sorry." He lined up quickly, but then the moon was gone. It's useless, I thought.

"What's that sound?" asked Johnno.

"What sound?"

We listened together, aware all at once of the stillness and the damp. There was a deep, slow, drumming sound in the water itself. We listened a long time, but it didn't vary. Then the foghorn sounded. It was a good deal closer.

"I don't know—"

"It's a ship," said Johnno, "and it's sounding its foghorn."

I ought to have known the sound of a ship's engines anywhere. We had heard them often through the water when we were in swimming. "She's travelling slowly," he said.

"We might be in her track."

Johnno brightened at this. 'She might pick us up! She might take us—"

"She'd hand us over to the pilot and the pilot would hand us to the police."

For a time he didn't answer, then he said wearily, "I dare say."

The drumming was clearer and the foghorn much louder, but it was hard to tell from which side the sounds came. In the bows Gyp was listening with his ears cocked, moving his head this way and that, making small worried sounds in his throat.

What did it matter if we were picked up, anyhow? Even Moloney was beginning to seem reasonable.

The drumming and the foghorn were growing louder. Gyp whined suddenly.

"Lie down," cried Johnno. "Hell, Charlie, they *might* give us to the police!"

"I don't reckon it matters much, anyhow."

"I can't go back. I'd rather swim for it."

We sat undecidedly while Gyp moved about in his small space. The moon uncovered again. It was behind us now. We didn't even bother to alter direction.

"It might run us down," I said.

But Johnno didn't care about that. All he could think of was the risk of being caught.

Gyp whined softly and shivered and crept close to Johnno's back. Johnno sat with the oars raised, his face strained, the corner of his mouth oozing blood, his eyes like black caverns. Now and then he dipped an oar feebly. "We're done for all right; done cold."

A few minutes more and the sound was all round us—a rhythmical drumming, like monstrous heart-beats, then the foghorn cry.

Gyp began whimpering.

"Oh, hell—shut up!" begged Johnno.

"It's that way," I said, pointing into the fog.

It was coming loudly, but still slowly and deliber-ately. I had to raise my voice above the drumming of it and when the foghorn came we were deafened.

"It's damn' close."

Gyp whined loudly. Suddenly the fog was cut apart and there, as high as a cliff, rose the bows of a liner. We stood up together.

"She's got us."

"Sit down," cried Johnno. He grabbed an oar and as the stem passed to one side of us, he pushed us away.

Rows of portholes passed like moons over our heads. Somewhere an orchestra was pounding, all out of time with the *drum, drum* of the engines. The foghorn blasted violently all around us.

Johnno went to push again, but the oar must have slipped. In a second he was on his back in the bottom of the boat and we were bumping the liner's side. I pushed with my hands and felt her rounded rivet heads on my palms. The next minute she was past and we were swirling and bobbing in her wake. I looked up and saw MALOJA — BELFAST on her stern, then the fog swallowed her and the drumming and hooting retreated.

Johnno regained his seat and we sat without speaking, half paralyzed with fright.

All at once Johnno sprang up. "The oars—we've lost both of them!"

We began looking about the small area of surface we could see in the fog, but there was nothing.

"I'm going over to look," said Johnno stripping off his trousers.

"No," I said in a shaky voice, "No; we'd get separated."

He put his face close to mine. "You know what'll happen if we don't get them? We'll get washed through the Heads clean out to sea."

I said quickly, "We mightn't be anywhere near the Heads."

"We've been rowing for hours and all the time the tide's been going out."

"If we're near the Heads we'd hear the surf."

We listened, but all we could hear was the retreating *drum, drum* of the ship and the blasting of its foghorn.

"There's a second foghorn," said Johnno suddenly. "Do they have one at the Heads?"

"I don't know," I said huskily.

"We've got to find the oars."

I said, "There's a rope in the locker—I could hang on to you."

I took it out, about twenty feet of it. He tied it round his waist and went over the stern. I played the line out and watched him disappear in the fog. Gyp stood in the bows, his head tilted this way and that, whimpering quietly. The day's happenings were tumbling through my mind—Johnno's composition, the inkpot, the crunch of Moloney's spectacles, Eileen coming . . . .

Distinctly I heard two foghorns.

"Charlie!"

"Yes?"

The rope had swung in a semicircle.

"I see an oar. Give us more rope."

"You've got it all." I leant out over the bows, jammed against Gyp.

"I touched it. No, no; it's gone, Charlie, it's moving fast . . . no good; I'm coming back."

I began pulling the rope, but it was like pulling dead weight.

"Johnno—you okay, Johnno?"

He panted something I couldn't hear. I drew harder and in a moment he appeared out of the fog, swimming strongly. He caught hold of the stern, and hung there panting, his lips drawn over his teeth.

"It's no good, Charlie. We're in a hell of a current."

He had hardly said it when a puff of wind came and all at once we were under stars with shore lights winking off to the left. A wall of shallow fog lay astern and the moon stood far down to the west. Ahead of us, about two miles off, was the *Maloja,* standing between two lights, one high and flashing white and red, the other steady white. We stared at them, not saying a word. "It's the Rip," I thought, "Nepean and Lonsdale, Nepean and Lonsdale, Nepean—"

"We'd stand a chance swimming—" began Johnno suddenly.

"No," I said.

He went on quickly without listening, "That place a bit behind us would be Portsea. We could angle across to allow for the current—"

"We'd never make it—"

"We could give it a go." He was standing up now. "If we don't we'll get washed clean out to sea."

Always, whatever happened in the water, Johnno was sure he could get out of it by swimming.

"We'd go through, anyhow. If we stick with the boat we've got a chance."

"What do we row with?"

I glanced round at the glittering sea, hoping wildly that an oar would drift alongside.

"We've *got* to swim, Charlie. Listen, I'll go in again and see what it's like swimming *across* the current—"

"You nearly got washed away before—"

"But *across* the current."

He waited no longer, but dived in without the rope and struck towards the shore, heading for the Portsea lights. Ten yards out he turned and trod water. When he did this I saw straight beyond his head a light flashing white and green on the shore. The two were lined up, his head and the light, then in a second they were apart, the light moving left and Johnno's head right.

"It's no good," I shouted. "You're drifting too fast."

He said nothing, but began swimming back. If I kept my eyes on him he looked to be going well, but when I looked beyond him, the few shore lights were slipping by quickly. I helped him over the stern again, his white barrel of a chest heaving in the moonlight.

"We've got to ride it out," he agreed hopelessly.

The boat now was rocking under us with quick, turning motions, the water hissing quietly along our sides.

"We're turning in a circle."

231

I looked and it was true. Slowly we swung away from the lights to the left, till we faced Point Lonsdale, then round farther till we faced the retreating fog, then right round back to Portsea. We circled slowly, then began again. I glanced back anxiously at Johnno. The sight of his face made me feel more than ever in a nightmare. The moon was full on him so that his blackened eyes looked like sockets. Naked as he was, his body wet, his hair matted, he looked like no one I had ever seen.

"We're going to miss Point Nepean."

"We could yell," I said.

"You do it."

"No—together."

We yelled for help a couple of times, then, bad as things were, we felt ashamed.

"I'd sooner drown," said Johnno bitterly.

The drumming of the *Maloja* had gone, but there was another sound, a sound like thunder a long way off. It was broken regularly by the blaring of the Lonsdale foghorn.

"I'm not scared of the surf," said Johnno, half to himself. "It's getting through the Rip."

"The *Cheviot*," I thought, "and the *Alert* and the *Corsair*—"

We were turning again, more swiftly now. The moon shone on great whorls of water to either side of us. In the bows Gyp began whimpering.

"Shut up," I begged. He came and licked my face. I pushed him away irritably.

Lonsdale swung past and the lights of Queenscliff, then the retreating fog up the bay. We completed the circle again, but this time more quickly. The water was almost silent except for the far noise of surf. Round again—Lonsdale, Queenscliff—

"Can a rowing-boat get through the Rip?"

When I tried to answer, saliva rose in my mouth and suddenly I was vomiting. I hung over the side unable to move, aware of Johnno behind me and of sudden peaks of water rising and subsiding around us, hissing in the moonlight and then of surf breaking on the very tip of Nepean. I gave up hope at that and clung whimpering to the side of the boat.

As I crouched there water burst over me, sending me sprawling backwards. At the same instant the boat rose on its beam ends.

"This is it, Charlie. Hang on to her!"

It was as if we were suspended in air, as if the Rip was deciding how to finish us. The moment ended with a tremendous jolt and water rushing in and the hissing of waves, much louder.

"Bale, Charlie!"

I was scrabbling for the tin when Johnno shouted, "Gyp's in!"

I forgot our danger; I forgot everything, I struggled to my knees and saw him swimming not far off, being twisted this way and that. I picked up the rope and flung an end to him, but it was too far off. He had his eyes on us, his head up high.

"Johnno, I'm going in."

"No!" shouted Johnno.

"He'll drown!"

"You can't—you wouldn't have a hope."

I stood up. "It's getting better; we're nearly through—"

But at that I found myself on my back in the bottom of the boat in sloshing water and Johnno standing over me, panting, "Jesus, Charlie, you couldn't live in it. We've got to bale!"

He picked up the tin and started at it frantically, but I struggled to my knees and looked back.

"He's still there," I said.

He still had his head up, but we were separating fast.

"He's gone—we'll never get him!"

"He'll swim to the beach."

"He'll try to follow me—he'd follow me anywhere."

I could see him only faintly now, then not at all, then a glimpse of him as the water turned him.

"He's gone, Johnno."

A faint bark followed my words, then nothing. I lay in the bottom of the boat with Johnno baling beside me and I cried and vomited and cried and vomited.

CHAPTER TWENTY-EIGHT

The stars had grown faint and there was no moon. A sick light was in the east. Johnno sat in the stern, naked still. We were rising and falling on a long regular swell. I straightened up and looked towards the coast. The Rip was far behind to the north-west with Point Lonsdale lighthouse winking palely. I looked hopelessly about for Gyp.

"We had him from a pup," I said.

Johnno looked up. "I'm sorry," he said. "Hell, I'm sorry. I should've gone in myself, but—Charlie, it was no go."

We didn't say anything more. The light was growing slowly, but the sun was not yet up; the sea was very dark blue. The swell lifted us, then rolled by. We were about half a mile offshore and were moving steadily down the coast towards Cape Schanck.

"He might swim it," said Johnno to himself. "He was part Labrador, wasn't he?"

"Labrador–Kelpie cross," I said.

We sat staring at the sea. "Your clothes have gone," I said. I had no idea when or where it had happened.

"It doesn't matter."

"You've got to wear something. Here." I took off my trousers and handed him my underpants.

"Thanks."

He put them on but they covered hardly any of him.

"What are we going to do?"

"We're drifting that way," he said. He pointed towards Cape Schanck. The waves there were slowly climbing the cliffs, spray was hanging, then falling back. There were other lower headlands nearer us; on them too the waves climbed slowly.

"If we get against those we're caught. We'd smash on rocks and get in the kelp."

The sun came up and glared on the water. The sea took on a different shade of blue. Directly over us a Pacific gull soared, moving its head as it looked down. By watching the shore I could see we were drifting fast towards the first headland, but also we were getting nearer the beach.

"We'll end up on the rocks," said Johnno. He looked at me seriously. "Charlie, we've *got* to swim this time, *got* to."

I answered, "We'd go on the rocks just the same."

"Swimming we'd be moving to the beach; in this we aren't."

I looked unhappily at the beach. It was clear what would happen: we would be pitched onto the first headland where the kelp and undertow would get us.

"What about the boat?"

Johnno looked worried. "Maybe it will wash up all right. If it gets smashed, it'd smash with us in it anyhow."

I saw that he was right. There was nothing for it but to swim.

"We'd better go, then," I said, taking off my shoes.

"You go first," said Johnno. "Make a line for the big dune, then you'll wash only about half-way to the rocks."

We didn't speak another word. I put off my shoes and went in over the stern and struck with long, slow strokes towards the dune. I could feel the ocean rise and fall under me and the steady side-drag of the current. I glanced back from the top of a wave and saw Johnno still standing in the boat. Next time I looked he had gone.

He's going between me and the rocks, I thought.

I didn't look again; I only raised my eyes occasionally to check the dune. Already, I was beginning to see less of the west side of it, more of the east. After ten minutes I looked round for Johnno but couldn't see him. I faced the dune again, and quickened my stroke. It was hardly two hundred yards now to the beach. I threw all my strength into it and quickened my kicking, but when I looked again the whole dune was hidden by tea-tree.

I found a tree higher than the rest and aimed then for it, but the current now was stronger and my trousers hung like legirons. Next time I lifted my head I heard clearly the roar of surf. I thought at first it was coming from the beach, then I saw I was scarcely a hundred yards off the headland. The water was boiling on the rocks, then drawing back over kelp. I angled sharply away from it, but as I turned I faced into the current. It halted me completely, then began to bear me in its own direction.

I angled again towards the shore. Then, between me and the rocks, only a few yards off, I saw Johnno, stroking confidently, turning his head sometimes my way, sometimes towards the rocks. Just ahead the waves were rising and turning over for their run to the beach. I caught a glimpse of Johnno picking one up and body-surfing over the last fifty yards. I tried and missed, then tried again and found myself soaring easily, the beach ahead. It almost seemed as if all our troubles were over.

Johnno ran to the place where I came in. I lay in the white wash hardly able to hold against the drag back. Before the next wave came I crawled to dry sand. Johnno sat beside me, breathing easily, saying nothing. The sun now was well up; the coast was wild and empty.

"We'd better watch for the boat—"

"Damn' the boat," I said.

I stood up, thinking to look for Gyp, but my legs crumpled and the sky fell in on me . . .

CHAPTER TWENTY-NINE

I was lying in speckled sunlight under tea-tree, the surf less loud, Johnno sitting beside me looking worried, his body all streaked with salt.

"What happened?"

"You fell over—tripped, I reckon."

"I passed out," I said bitterly. I didn't ask how I had got there; assumption was embarrassing enough.

"Listen, there's Gyp and the boat—"

"To hell with the boat," I said irritably. "Why are you always—"

"Well, Gyp—"

"I'll come," I said.

He looked at me doubtfully. I stood up, but the clouds spun and the horizon tilted horribly. I dropped to my hands and knees and began vomiting in the sand.

"Maybe I'd better go."

When I didn't answer, he went away over the dunes.

I was too exhausted even to wonder about the future. Out of the wind the sun was warm. I lay down again and fell asleep.

Johnno was sitting beside me studying a stick he had put upright on a bit of flattened sand. I started to speak to him, but my throat was so dry that I only raised a croaking. He said, "The shadows are getting longer—it's past midday—"

"Find Gyp?"

He shook his head. "He might have made for home." He looked away from me. "Charlie, the boat's jammed in the rocks. She'll be smashed to bits—"

I said indifferently, "I don't care. All I want is a drink."

He reached behind him in the shade and handed me a beach bucket half full. "It's got wrigglers in it—it came from a tank at a house." He moved his head inland.

I drank greedily. "Did you see anyone?"

"No one."

I looked at him—cut cheek, black eyes, bruises where his father had hit him about the ribs, nothing more on than my underpants. "Just as well," I said.

We were alive and the sun was warm. I could almost have been happy had we had Gyp.

"Would he try to follow the boat, or would he go for the shore?"

"The current would take him the way it took us, I reckon."

"No tracks near the boat?"

Johnno shook his head dismally. "No tracks at all."

"We could look the other way."

I stood up stiffly and we started over the dunes, meeting the roar of sea and a fresh wind from the south. Up the beach I could see the boat jammed on the headland, but the other way there was nothing, not even a footprint. We walked slowly for half a mile, always looking for pad marks and now and then stopping and whistling.

"He'd never hear us," I said.

We were turning back when I saw something that looked like a heap of seaweed darker than the rest. Neither of us said anything, but when I went to walk to it Johnno said, "Maybe we should go back."

I didn't answer him; instead I began hurrying. Well before I reached the place I could see Gyp lying on his side, the way he always lay by our fire. When I reached him and looked at him I saw that there wasn't a mark on him. I touched his ear, but it was cold.

I jumped up and cried, "Curse your bloody running away."

Johnno stood with his arms hanging by his side, muttering, "Sorry, Charlie; sorry."

I dragged Gyp up into the dunes and scooped sand over him. When I stood up I said, "I shouldn't have said that. It could have been me drowned."

Johnno turned away. "I wish it had been me," he said.

I didn't know what I had expected running away from home to be like—certainly not like this, anyhow. Perhaps I had imagined a train journey somewhere and farmers offering meals without asking questions. It was twenty-four hours since the inkwell incident. It didn't seem to me that we were any better off.

"They'll think we're dead," said Johnno. We were walking back to our place in the tea-tree. "I didn't mean to upset my old man and Eileen as badly as that."

"Perhaps it's better that way."

"Better?"

"When they hear we're alive they'll be so pleased that nothing will be done to us. What we've got to do is wait till morning, then find a telephone—"

Johnno stopped walking and looked at me, his salt hair standing on end in the wind. "Charlie, if I went back it'd be a reformatory this time."

"Your father would be glad—"

"No, Charlie; not me. No going back—"

He looked so alarmed that I decided to talk no more about it.

"You *want* to go back?"

"I don't know," I said uneasily. "Anyhow, what we've got to do first is find food."

I don't know where I thought we would find food. When we went back to the water bucket, I remembered that we weren't fit to be seen; at least Johnno certainly wasn't.

I said, "If I went and asked for food somewhere—"

"You can't," Johnno interrupted. "Gawd, Charlie, you look terrible! People would ask what had happened."

"But we've got to eat and you've got to get clothes—well, trousers, anyhow."

He began pouring sand agitatedly through his fingers. "There's the house where I got the water—"

"What's it like?"

"A week-end house; no one been there for months. But, Charlie, we can't break in. Everything there belongs to someone else."

"What do we do, then? Walk up Point Nepean Road barefooted—you in my underpants?"

"I don't know; fair dinkum, Charlie, it's not the way I expected."

"Let's *look* at the house, anyhow."

He stood up reluctantly, his stomach gurgling with hunger. "All right, then."

The house was in scrub not far behind the beach; a small, sad, squarish place with tea-tree branches hanging over it. Its roof was rusted and its windows were covered with salt and dust. On a rack under the tank-stand were three long bamboo fishing-rods. Except for Johnno's earlier footprints and a few rabbit tracks, there wasn't a mark to be seen. At the front was a low veranda. We stepped on it and tried the front door, but as we had expected, it was locked.

"We could try the back."

"I tried it before."

"The windows, then."

We went round the house, pushing at them. "We could smash one," I said.

"Do we have to? It's someone's house." I walked away from him and began running my fingers round various ledges. It was no good.

"Where else would they keep the key?"

"They probably take it home."

"Well, we *will* smash a window, then."

"No," said Johnno, "No. Not yet, anyhow."

He had walked back to the tank-stand and was looking underneath. I heard him say, "This might be it." He unhooked something from a nail. "At any rate it's a key."

He tried the back door and it opened unwillingly. An odour met us of rooms a long time shut.

CHAPTER THIRTY

When the door closed behind us the sea sounded farther off, rolling and breaking in one long roar. We stood waiting for our eyes to become accustomed to the light, neither of us speaking a word. I felt the house listening and watching, just as we were listening and watching. We stood in a long room—a kitchen, living-room and dining-room all in one. A wood stove was at one end and near it a table.

"I don't like it," said Johnno in a low voice.

"Don't like what?"

"Being here."

I didn't answer, but walked quietly round the rest of the house. There was a small bathroom, and two bedrooms each with two beds and mattresses. Blankets were stacked in a wardrobe.

I came back to Johnno.

"Look," he said.

He was pointing to a map of the Peninsula pinned to a wall. On the beach behind Rye someone had pencilled a cross and had marked OUR PLACE.

"We'd better find food," I said.

Though his stomach had hardly stopped gurgling, Johnno looked at me as if I had suggested murdering someone.

"*I'm* going to eat anyhow," I said.

He followed me unhappily while I opened cupboards. The only thing in the house was rolled oats—about a pound of it. Once he had seen it Johnno stared at it hungrily.

"We've got to find matches."

We began a search, but there were none in the house.

"You can eat it as it is," said Johnno, nibbling a bit.

"Or it could soak in cold water," I suggested. "My mother soaks it overnight."

I took out a saucepan and tipped about half a pound into it. "It's got worms in it."

"They'll only taste like oatmeal," said Johnno indifferently. "I'll get the water."

He turned on a tap over the sink. Rusty water flowed for a minute or two, then cleared.

Johnno watched me trying to pick out worms. "What's the use?" he asked. "The water's full of wrigglers anyhow."

So we mixed the oatmeal and water with a spoon, then I sat back and looked at it, hoping some miracle might turn it into porridge.

"Well?" said Johnno.

"You can have first spoonful," I said.

He scooped at it, worms and wrigglers and oatmeal, and put them in his mouth.

"It's good."

I scooped at it with my eyes closed. It was bearable if I didn't think about it. We ate spoonful for spoonful till we had finished, then we sat looking at the empty saucepan.

"We'd better save some till morning," I said.

Johnno washed the saucepan and spoon and put them away, then we sat at the table trying to pretend we were satisfied, that the situation wasn't bad at all. Every now and then Johnno got up and studied the map, but each time he shook his head despondently. The light was fading still further and the wind was springing up, setting twigs and branches scraping the walls. The sea was louder and more threatening.

"It'll smash the boat," said Johnno.

"Ah, shut up about the boat!" I said.

He fell into a mournful silence, staring at the floor, looking more depressed than ever, gooseflesh on his bare back, his face a mess of cuts and bruises. I began to feel sorry for him and was about to say something when he flung his head up.

"That was a shot."

"I didn't hear anything."

He looked less certain.

"With the noise of the waves," I added, "I don't see how you'd hear it."

"Maybe not. They wouldn't have guns anyhow."

"Who?"

"The police."

"They probably don't even know."

He looked doubtful, but we settled to uneasy silence again. The sun was behind the tea-tree by this and the room was becoming gloomier and full of sea sounds.

"It'd be better on the veranda," I said. "These rooms give me the creeps."

We stood up slowly, as if someone had been watching us.

"Perhaps you'd better wrap a blanket round yourself," I told him.

"Well, the blankets really belong to someone else—"

"Hell!" I cried, "We'll have to borrow them tonight anyhow."

Johnno frowned. "I'm not cold."

"It's the way you look that I'm thinking of—those underpants hardly cover your backside."

"No one's going to see us, are they?"

I supposed not. We went drearily outside. The veranda faced west and one corner still caught a few rays of sunshine. Out there the sea was much louder, its cries more threatening.

The veranda was boarded in to about waist height; blinds could be pulled down to make a sleep-out. We leant on the rail, staring at the clumps of tea-tree and blackwood and the open spaces between.

"There are rabbits here, anyhow," said Johnno, as if rabbits were going to provide food for us for weeks.

"We can run them down and eat them raw," I said bitterly.

He looked at me from the corner of his eye. "Fair dinkum, Charlie, I didn't mean to get you into this."

I was beginning to feel regretful for being impatient with him, when from somewhere behind the tea-tree came the crack of a rifle. At the same instant Johnno fell to the floor, face down. Before I could hide myself a girl appeared about fifty yards off with a repeating rifle in her hand.

I leant down quickly. "Johnno, are you hurt?"

He didn't move. I bent closer in a panic, grasping his arm, "Fred—"

"Get down or you'll be seen," he hissed.

At that I wanted to kick him. "I've been seen," I answered.

He groaned quietly, his face to the floor. "It's only a girl, anyhow," I said.

It's useless to move, I thought; better to be casual.

But I had never been casual with girls, not even in school.

She had stopped and was standing less than twenty yards off, the rifle under her arm. She looked about fourteen, a fairish girl with one sun-bleached plait. She was looking straight at me with a puzzled expression, her manner not showing any concern at all.

I said, "G'day."

"Oh, hullo," she answered, standing still. She was barefooted and wearing a faded cotton dress. "Are you on holidays here?"

"Sort of," I said.

Johnno tapped my ankle. "Don't tell her anything."

"Shut up!" I said, turning my head away.

"Pardon?" said the girl, moving nearer.

"A sort of a holiday," I repeated. "Only a day or two."

"You must be a friend of the Edwards?"

"My mother is," I said uncomfortably.

Johnno touched my ankle again. I kicked him and muttered something.

"Pardon?" said the girl again, coming nearer.

"Nothing," I said dumbly. We stared awhile at each other. She had wide-open disconcerting eyes.

"Are your mother and father down?"

251

"Tell her yes," whispered Johnno.

"They're coming tonight."

"How did you get down then?"

I heard Johnno moan. I waved my hand vaguely. "We got a ride—"

"You have friends with you then?"

"My brother's down," I said, quickly, "but he's in swimming."

She was about ten yards off now, the rifle in the crook of her bare arm, the wind blowing her plait about. She said, "It's a very dangerous beach here, you know."

"Yes," I said, "but he's a good swimmer."

At my feet Johnno hissed desperately, "Stop talking."

"Who was that?" asked the girl, listening suddenly.

"No one," I answered. "I didn't hear anything."

She looked at me closely. I noticed her expression change as if a realization had hit her. She said slowly, "Are you one of the boys?"

"What boys?"

"The two who ran away and took a boat—it came over the wireless. I forget their names. What's your name?"

"Smith," whispered Johnno.

"Smith," I faltered.

She looked grave. "That's not true, of course. That's what everyone says when they don't want to give their real name. What *is* your name?"

"I've told you," I said unsteadily.

"Well, I don't believe you. Anyhow," she went on, "I wouldn't tell anyone even if I did know. I think running away would be terrific."

We stared at each other again in a dumb battle which lasted minutes on end. She swung the rifle carelessly from side to side. On the floor Johnno said hoarsely, "Has she gone?"

The girl had come farther forward. "That's the other boy!" she exclaimed triumphantly.

"No," I said weakly.

She came still nearer. I stepped quickly off the veranda to try to divert her.

"Now you'll make up some story to the police—" I began.

"Of course I won't. Where are you running away to?"

I opened my mouth to say I wasn't running away but just then the colour left her face and I felt she was going to collapse. Following her gaze I saw Johnno looking over the veranda rail, only his head showing, a head so knocked about that it looked like something guillotined a few days before.

"It's no good, Charlie." The voice sounded not much better than a guillotined head could be expected to sound.

The girl came over and stood close to me. "Who is it?"

"Johnno," I said wearily. "We were washed through the Rip. We haven't had any food and Johnno has hardly any clothes."

"Is he all right?"

"Right enough."

"How did he get so hurt?"

"On the rocks," croaked Johnno.

She came closer and peered at the head. Her colour was coming back quickly.

"Terrific," she murmured.

Johnno rolled his eyes towards me like a dog.

"He needs more clothes," I said.

"I'll come back with some," she answered firmly. "Stand up while I see how big you are."

The head shook determinedly.

"He's six feet two," I told her.

"Terrific," said the girl again.

We waited uneasily for her decision. "I'll come back after tea. I'll knock at the door and say the password—"

"What password?"

"We must decide one."

Johnno looked at me despairingly.

"We might be out," I said quickly. "Yes, we'd be safer in the bush. But we'll come back after dark. Leave the things under the tank-stand, then we'll know where to find them."

She looked disappointed. "But I wouldn't see you."

"Well—the police might follow you."

After a bit she said reluctantly, "Oh, all right then."

We stood watching her go away the way she had come. She turned and waved once. I waved back, but Johnno didn't move.

CHAPTER THIRTY-ONE

When the girl had disappeared from sight Johnno sat on the veranda steps, his head in his hands. "That's done it."

"Well, what would you have said?"

"I don't know," he admitted. "You just can't trust them, though. We'd better clear out, or she'll get some mad idea like wanting to come with us."

I went inside and took four blankets and we walked into the scrub on the side of the dunes. From there we could see part of the house and the tank-stand and anyone approaching. The waves had grown much louder and dusk was coming early. We wrapped ourselves up and lay on our stomachs watching the house carefully. Lying that way seemed to ease our hunger. We lay there about two hours in gloomy light, scarcely speaking.

The moon was already up when we saw the girl coming back carrying a bundle. She came slowly towards the tank-stand and stooped there. Then she straightened up and gazed around.

"Her old man'll come," whispered Johnno. "Sure to. If it was Eileen, my old man would be moving in now with a bike chain."

But he was wrong; no one came. The girl turned round and began walking back, stopping every so often to look towards the house. Before long she disappeared into the shadows.

"A pretty good kid, after all," I said, standing up.

"Sit down," whispered Johnno. "It's a trap."

I sank back again and we kept watching. We watched for an hour or more, then went singly to the house, keeping in the shadows.

In the bundle were half a dozen scones, a leg of mutton only half finished, some roast potatoes, still warm, and a jar of milk. They were wrapped in a pair of trousers and a sweater.

"There's a note in it."

We held the piece of paper to the moon. "Can't read it," said Johnno, tilting it this way and that.

He handed it to me, but I could do no better.

"Might be a warning."

"Keep it till morning," I said.

We went back into the scrub and ate like jungle animals at a carcass. Then Johnno dressed himself.

Except for his hair and his face and the fact that he had nothing on his feet, he looked reasonably civilized.

"We can't walk far without boots."

"Why?"

"People would notice us—"

"At night they wouldn't."

I hadn't thought of walking at night.

"By tomorrow morning we could cover about twenty miles."

I supposed so, but without any keenness. All I wanted was sleep, yet here was Johnno who hadn't slept at all, wanting to walk twenty miles barefoot.

"Where would twenty miles put us, anyway? It would only take us nearer home."

"We could go towards the Western Port side and make for the railway."

Against this idea I could think of no real argument. I said feebly, "Let's have a night's sleep, anyhow."

Johnno frowned. "If we wait around here he'll find us before—"

"Who will?"

"My old man."

"Ah, to hell with your old man," I said bitterly.

"But—"

"All right then," I said wearily. "You lead the way—I bet you don't even know which way to head."

But I was wrong. He had studied the map at the house more fully than I had known.

"We go along the beach to the next point, then inland from there by a road. That takes us to another road that goes to Shoreham—"

I turned away from him. I still had the mutton bone in my hand, all bare and white after our gnawing. I dug a hole and buried it. I was hardly better than a dog, I thought, and certainly worse off than the Prodigal Son. Somehow I couldn't imagine Johnno's father killing any fatted calf. My own father—yes, I could imagine him.

We walked over the top of the dunes into a fresh wind and the roar of waves. The sea glittered and moved in the moonlight, but sometimes clouds darkened it and all the expanse of beach darkened too. Then the clouds would race away again as if hurrying to report our whereabouts.

Beside me Johnno said, "It'll be better walking near the water."

Down there the roar was louder so that we seemed back again in the battle of the past night. Only Gyp was missing. If I saw Ian again, I thought, what could I tell him?

Between us and the rocky headland the moon shone on wet sand. Waves ran over it, white and aggressive, then fell back with gasping sounds. Before us, away beyond the headland, the Cape Schanck light flashed brightly.

"We should walk fast," urged Johnno above the noise.

"I am walking fast," I said irritably. I wanted only to lie down.

Cape Schanck dropped out of sight behind the headland. Just then a cloud passed over the moon and the brightness drained out of the night. I shivered and took longer strides to keep up with Johnno. He was still a pace or two in front of me when I saw him stop. When I caught up he said, "There are lights ahead coming over the dunes."

We stood close together watching them.

"We'd better go back to the tea-tree."

We scrambled up the beach and lay on the crest of a dune. From there we could see five or six lights bobbing in single file and behind them the lights of a car.

"They're at the end of the road we have to take," said Johnno.

"Someone has found the boat, then."

"The girl probably told her father about us."

"No," I said. "No—she'd only have got herself into trouble."

We began pushing through the tea-tree, with the idea of passing behind the searchers and going up the road. The moon came out again, brightening the whole beach and on it a group of men at the water's edge. They stood there looking. After a few minutes they turned and went back to the cars.

"They're going away," said Johnno.

But they didn't go away. When we came closer we could see a dinghy on a trailer and this they began unloading. The wind blew from them to us, but their voices reached us indistinctly.

"Charlie, we'd better beat it," said Johnno. But he made no attempt to move.

"They're going to row to where the boat hit the rocks," I said.

"They'll get caught," said Johnno anxiously.

We moved through heavy shadows till we were scarcely twenty yards from them, then we dropped on our hands and knees and crawled through the scrub. The men now were very close. We wormed towards them on our stomachs as they began carrying the dinghy to the beach. In front of them a man and a woman carried hurricane lamps.

I caught Johnno's arm. "That's Eileen and your dad."

I heard him moan. But then he whispered, "I can't go back, Charlie."

Old man Johnston was bowed and shrunken-looking; he shambled along in a hopeless sort of way.

As we watched, the wind brought someone's voice to us, ". . . in by the flat rock . . . ."

Johnno looked away. "I can't do this to him. Could we shout that we're okay, then run for it?"

"I dare say," I said unhappily.

"Hell, Charlie, I didn't mean it to work out this way!"

261

The group was down at the water now. On the road I heard a car door slam and there, standing together, were my mother and father, my father half holding my mother up.

I almost leapt out. Johnno hung on to my arm suddenly.

"It's no good," I said, "I've got to speak to them."

"Give me just two minutes, Charlie—just one minute—"

"You've got to come with me."

"No," he said, "I can't. Tell my old man I left you. Tell him—tell him—"

He got to his knees.

"It's no good," I said again. "You've nowhere to go."

But he had turned round and was beginning to crawl through the tea-tree.

At the water's edge there was a shot and sudden brilliant light. The silhouettes of the men showed up against the bright sea. Out farther were the rocks with waves running over them and there, still held fast, the smashed boat. Over everything hung the dazzling flare. I looked quickly back and saw my mother leaning against my father still. Then it was dark again.

"Johnno," I said, "I'm going out."

But Johnno was gone.

"Johnno!" I repeated.

I looked into the bush after him, but now it was black. Above the noise of waves I could catch no sound of him. I felt the courage run suddenly out of me, but I stood up slowly and walked out of the bush as if it had all been a dream.

I was close to them before my mother and father saw me. We stared at each other, then I said, "We're all right."

My father lifted his hand, then let it fall again. He said nothing.

"Fred?" asked my mother.

"He's safe," I said.

At that she collapsed. I stood fixed to the spot while my father struggled to get her into the car. In a voice unlike his own he said, "Tell Mr Johnston."

I began running to the water's edge, calling out something as I ran. They had the dinghy now a little way out to sea. I saw Mr Johnston and Eileen standing together like two pieces of stone.

"He's safe!" I shouted.

Eileen swung round and grasped me by both arms. "Where is he?"

Her father scarcely seemed to have heard me. He had the same shrunken, distant look about him.

"He left me," I said.

"When?"

At that I forgot all our caution, "A few minutes ago."

"We must tell the police," said Eileen quickly.

"No," said her father, arousing himself. "No. He's alive and that's all that matters. He'll come back if he wants to come back."

That was the end of it all. On the drive home no one talked about it; in fact, no one talked about anything. I looked at first into the roadside scrub thinking I might see Johnno, but before long we were well beyond his range and by ten o'clock we were home, all staring at each other, not speaking, not believing it had happened.

CHAPTER THIRTY-TWO

That was the end of Johnno's days in Kananook, the end too of 1929. In January we were to move out of "Thermopylae". Always I was to link it with Johnno and the death of Grandfather McDonald and all the other happenings of the year.

With Johnno gone and Gyp dead and a cloud of disgrace over me, the holidays were not worth having. Only one happening brightened them.

One night I was alone at the end of the pier, sitting there dangling my legs over the edge. It was warm and the sea was calm, but I was thinking of the day Johnno and I had got our Bronze Medallions and of the storm and the wreck during the next night. It all seemed years ago. I began thinking how good it would be if Johnno could turn up when, at that moment, someone did drop down beside me and say, "Ah there, Charlie."

I looked and it was Squid. "I was thinking of Johnno," I said disappointedly.

He didn't answer. When I looked at him again I could have sworn he'd been crying.

"What's up?" I asked, not really caring much.

He lay on his back looking at the stars, still not answering.

"I don't see what you've got to be gloomy about," I said bitterly. "You're not in trouble; you won the Most Improved Pupil again; old Moloney loves you—"

"Don't say that," he exclaimed, his voice quavery.

"Why?"

"Because—well—" He turned on his side and looked away from me. "They've just told me—him and my mother—they're getting married—"

I suppose I should have expected it, but I hadn't. I swung round to him. "They're *what*?"

"It's true," he jerked out. "Before Christmas—all living together—"

It was too much; I burst out laughing. I hadn't laughed for a long time and I couldn't stop. I lay on my back while he begged and blubbered beside me. After, I felt ashamed; even Squid didn't deserve Moloney for a father.

A fortnight after this they were married as he had said. I wanted to write about it to Johnno, but

I didn't know where he was; no one knew where he was.

Somehow I hardly had Johnno out of my mind in those last days of the year. On New Year's Eve I decided to walk across the school ground to Lone Pine. But it was no good. The school looked shrunken and wasn't important any more; even Lone Pine wasn't the same. Perhaps if Johnno had come back it might have been the way it was before; without him it was nothing.

The Beginnings of
All the Green Year
by Don Charlwood

IMPROBABLE as it may seem, *All the Green Year* arose from a heated argument around our Templestowe dining-room table in the days when The Beatles came to Melbourne. Seated with me were my wife, our three daughters—one too young to be much interested in The Beatles, the other two both teenagers—and my elderly father-in-law. I sat at one end of the table, my wife on my right and at the far end her aged father, who was very deaf and involved in his own ruminations. (It was he who became the narrator's grandfather, Captain McDonald, in *All the Green Year*.)

In the middle of my arguments against going to The Beatles, my father-in-law suddenly roared, 'The Americans should get out of Vietnam!'

I shouted, 'Yes, they should get out!' Then, 'No, you can't go to The Beatles!' Feeling at the end of my tether, I turned to the eldest of the girls, saying, 'I've a good mind to put you two in a book!'

She retorted, 'What would you know about it, anyway?'

For a second I was nettled by her impertinence, then I realised she was right: I knew little about bringing up teenage girls, for I came from a family of four boys. I decided on the spot to write a novel about boys of about the same age as my daughters.

It took me four years to complete the book, as I had a heavy job with the Department of Civil Aviation: I was responsible for choosing men for Air Traffic Control, selecting both in Australia and in Britain. At least I had a start: the ABC had already read my tale of riding with Squid to school on a camel. Squid was based on a boy who lived next door to us in Frankston, a conman in the making.

The novel-to-be would be set in the small town of Frankston, thinly disguised as Kananook, in 1929, the year I turned fourteen. By then I had already suffered the schoolmaster on whom the character Moloney is based. I also had a London-born grandmother living in an East Melbourne home like the one mentioned in the book. But of the happenings in the story, only one actually took place: I witnessed the wreck of the small pleasure schooner *Isis,* but saw no one swim out to her.

Also the dog Gyp, who drowned in *All the Green Year*, was our very-much-alive dog while I was writing.

In my school days at Frankston Primary School No. 1464 the playing area was large, with remnants of high original pine trees and acres of bush lying beyond. In our grade was a boy named Jack Smythe, who was older and much taller than any of us. He was of slightly gingerish complexion and was full of yarns about faraway places. He enjoyed boxing and tried to teach me—not very successfully. He went on with me to the Frankston and District High School, the only school on the Mornington Peninsula where students could matriculate. Though Frankston itself did not number much over two thousand people, buses ran students from as far away as Portsea.

Jack wrote a few lines of verse for the Frankston High School magazine about the encumbrances of his new life:

> Another thing I do abhor
> Is when the term report is bad
> And you have to take the thing along
> And show it to your dad.

His dad was said to be a formidable man, though I don't remember ever seeing him. The local paper reported how skilfully he had defended himself in court on a minor charge: he had put the opposing counsel to flight. Jack was clearly afraid of him, which, for so big a boy, always seemed strange to me. He did not last long at high school. For a time he worked locally at labouring jobs, then he simply disappeared. His three elder sisters remained—all beautiful girls—but none of the family knew where Jack had gone. I never imagined then that some twenty-four years later I would make him the main character in a novel.

While thinking of the book's theme I happened to read a reviewer's remark that there was little humorous writing about Australian boyhood. This led me to re-use the camel ride with Squid, then dream up the events arising from the bullfight at the familiar Frankston pound. But I wanted to go beyond humour. The conflicts in my own domestic life could find outlet were I to write the story of one year in a boy's life, not only the humour of it but its drama and pain.

As the narrator of the story, I felt myself to be not only Charlie, but also Charlie's father. In one role I was more or less myself when young; in the other myself some thirty-five years later—a harassed father trying to pass on values once passed on to me. I would call the book *Johnno's Year*, with Jack Smythe mostly in mind as Johnno.

In a way 1929 was the end of an era. Until 1930 Australians seldom heard the American accent, but then came talking pictures. Previously Hollywood films had been silent; 'mood music' was provided—piano and flute in Frankston. Now alien speech poured into our ears: in musicals, westerns, gang warfare, smart comedy. Implicit in my story of boyhood in 1929 would be the suggestion that our era had been much less Americanised than those to come.

With 1929 decided upon, I made pages of notes on the impedimenta that formed the background to our lives in those days: gramophones, cable trams, coppers for boiling clothes, blacksmiths, jazz garters, milk dipped by milkmen into billies outside every gate, and early, crackling radio. As an aid to my memory I read 1929 newspapers and discussed the era with others who had also lived through it. I think this research led Professor A. R. Chisholm of the University of Melbourne to remark in a 1966 review of the finished book: 'His notations are so exact that I wonder whether this is a book of reminiscences skilfully retouched.'

I decided to relate the story in the first person, from the viewpoint of a secondary character; the main character would be Johnno. My sequence of happenings—grave, happy, hilarious—would be among a group of characters typical of my era. It was evident enough that the story would have to be larger than life to be worth relating; that more would happen in one year than would normally happen.

In 1962 I began writing. After a few pages I found myself baffled. My predicament will be clear from a series of questions I wrote down and tried to answer:

273

'1. Are you writing as a boy relating his own story? If so, what sort of a boy?—Intelligent? Sensitive? Or a sardonic dinkum Aussie?

'2. Or are you relating the story as a man looking back on his boyhood, recalling its scenes and conversations, but able to use adult terminology, an adult approach? If so, what sort of a man? Again, intelligent? Sensitive? Sardonic?

'3. Or are you at an intermediate age? A youth of twenty or so with recent memories of boyhood. If so, what sort of a youth, etc?

'No. 1. Writing as a boy limits you in vocabulary— which might not be a bad thing—but more seriously it limits you in maturity of observation, reflection, awareness. You cannot juxtapose happening A and happening B because the juxtaposition is howlingly funny, when only as an adult would you recognise its humour. True, this can chance to happen, but after several of these "chances" the reader feels doubtful of authenticity—as I often did in reading *Huckleberry Finn*. Too often I felt, "Here is an adult trying to be funny by posing as a boy and saying things he was only likely to have thought of as an adult."

'No. 2. Writing as a man looking back presents fewer limitations, but less immediacy. It can only be brought off if the man reveals himself infrequently and for the rest of the time relishes being a boy again. Alan Marshall does this well in *I Can Jump Puddles*. A man has looked back but his boyhood has repossessed him and he is only an adult when he needs an adult's expanded vision, or wisdom, or power of sentence construction.

'No. 3. Writing as a youth not long away from boyhood: I don't know that much really separates this from writing as a man—not enough, anyway, for me to make the effort of returning to two earlier stages of life instead of one.

'So I would elect to be a man looking back. What manner of man? Does this not in part depend on what I wish to depict? I want to depict the dry, blustering, rather hard Australian boy; but I also want to depict countryside, a little history, some drama and thought. The two don't go together. I, the narrator, therefore cannot be the typical Australian boy. I can observe the typical Australian boy. With the herd I can—as boys do—behave like the herd. Alone I can reflect.

'This shall be it then; look back as a man, but as a man who inwardly was not dry, sardonic, tough, even though he tried to conform to this Australian concept. Show, in fact, both sides, the sensitive and the tough.'

With my questions answered, the going became much easier.

While in Melbourne I wrote during lunch hours in the RACV men's reading room and in the evenings on the dining-room table at home, interrupted often by homework and parent–teenage encounters of the very sort I was attempting to depict. I also wrote in aeroplanes, and in various hotels—both in Australia and Britain. I mention these things because I began to feel that my disjointed life was resulting in a disjointed book. But I always enjoyed the writing of it.

Fortunately my wife had become adept in bringing order to my much-corrected pencil originals through having typed *No Moon Tonight*, my factual Bomber Command book. Early in 1964 she completed the second draft of the book. This I corrected in a Cairns motel. Soon afterwards I had to leave again for England. I left the corrected manuscript at home, telling my wife that I would need yet another draft to work on before a final version was submitted to a publisher. Some four months later, just before I left England to return to Melbourne, the manuscript unexpectedly reached me; with it a wifely ultimatum: 'I believe this is ready for a publisher. I have cut out the last sentence.' In this sentence I had told that Johnno had sent money to my father to pay for the boat he had lost. I agreed at once with this deletion. It was better for the reader to reach out with his own suppositions.

My wife's decision was vindicated. Being in London I left the manuscript with the agent who had handled

No Moon Tonight. It was accepted soon afterwards by Angus & Robertson, London. Because I had not carried out my intended final checking, some names of Frankston people of bygone years and names of actual places remained in the story. I had used them because they came easily to me as I wrote. Geographically I had had to move the town well south of the actual Frankston in order that the Heads episode would be feasible. (The credibility of this episode I had verified with an expert on the seas of Port Phillip and the Rip.)

The manuscript went to that formidable editor Beatrice Davis, at the Sydney office of Angus & Robertson, who sought no change to it beyond telling me that Caruso and Melba were never in Melbourne together. However, she asked that the title *Johnno's Year* be changed. This proved a laborious business.

With the book in print, two of Australia's foremost critics, A. A. Phillips and Beatrice Davis herself, had similar comments to make. Both felt that the first part read as a book about boys; the second part—the flight from home—as a book for boys. I could only reply that I was writing as an adult repossessed by boyhood and that the state of 'repossession' intensified as the book neared its climax, so that, briefly, I shed my age and became in spirit a boy again. At least, this is what I hoped I had achieved.

To return again to our Templestowe home: a call came to me from a University High School English teacher, Vaughan Hutchings. Complimenting me on the book, he began reading extracts to me, saying, 'That's just how boys of that age speak!' He then came quickly to the point: 'How do I get it set for schools?' I could only suggest contacting Beatrice Davis, little imagining that this would lead to the novel being read in schools for twenty years.

Having been medically retired from DCA at fifty-nine I was free to accept requests to speak at schools—and there were many. One year I was writer-in-residence at Tintern Church of England Girls' Grammar School, and an extraordinary exchange occurred. During a lunchbreak an English teacher, Jan O'Neill, asked, 'On what character is Johnno based?'

I told her he was based on three different boys I had known, but mainly on one named Jack Smythe.

To my astonishment she answered, 'He is my uncle.'

After a moment I asked, 'What happened to Jack?'

She said simply, 'We don't know.'

Years later Jan O'Neill was able to tell me that his grave had been found on Thursday Island. Much of his life had been spent in the Torres Strait Islands, in what capacity she was not sure. He died in 2006, aged ninety-three, on Horne Island, off Thursday Island. In 2012 Jack Smythe's nephew told me he believed his uncle passed on building skills to the young men of the islands.

April 2012

Text Classics

The Commandant
Jessica Anderson
Introduced by Carmen Callil

Homesickness
Murray Bail
Introduced by Peter Conrad

Sydney Bridge Upside Down
David Ballantyne
Introduced by Kate De Goldi

A Difficult Young Man
Martin Boyd
Introduced by Sonya Hartnett

The Australian Ugliness
Robin Boyd
Introduced by Christos Tsiolkas

All the Green Year
Don Charlwood
Introduced by Michael McGirr

The Even More Complete
Book of Australian Verse
John Clarke
Introduced by John Clarke

Diary of a Bad Year
JM Coetzee
Introduced by Peter Goldsworthy

Wake in Fright
Kenneth Cook
Introduced by Peter Temple

The Dying Trade
Peter Corris
Introduced by Charles Waterstreet

They're a Weird Mob
Nino Culotta
Introduced by Jacinta Tynan

Careful, He Might Hear You
Sumner Locke Elliott
Introduced by Robyn Nevin

Terra Australis
Matthew Flinders
Introduced by Tim Flannery

My Brilliant Career
Miles Franklin
Introduced by Jennifer Byrne

Cosmo Cosmolino
Helen Garner
Introduced by Ramona Koval

Dark Places
Kate Grenville
Introduced by Louise Adler

The Watch Tower
Elizabeth Harrower
Introduced by Joan London

The Mystery of
a Hansom Cab
Fergus Hume
Introduced by Simon Caterson

The Glass Canoe
David Ireland
Introduced by Nicolas Rothwell

The Jerilderie Letter
Ned Kelly
Introduced by Alex McDermott

For more information visit textclassics.com.au